The Guardian's Heart

Michel Prince

The Growing Strong Series
Book 1

The child's parents are not his makers but his guardians.
—Maria Montessori

God does not play dice with the universe.
—Albert Einstein

s

Published by
Satin Romance
An Imprint of Melange Books, LLC
White Bear Lake, MN 55110
www.satinromance.com

ISBN: 978-1-68046-299-9

Cover Art by Ashley Nguyen Photography
All cover art and logo copyright © Melange Books, LLC

This book, like all mine, is first and foremost dedicated to my husband, if for no other reason than he's always been the Guardian of my heart.

Secondly to April, Anita, Irene and Laura who helped me with their encouragement and support.

Finally, to my girl Ashley for helping me design the cover and my cover models, Braylyne and Mikale with their little cute butts. You guys were perfect.

The author acknowledges the trademark status and the following trademark owners mentioned in this work of fiction.

NBA-National Basketball Association NBA Media Ventures, LLC
Huggies-Kimberly-Clark Worldwide, Inc
McDonald's- McDonald's
Pampers-Proctor & Gamble
Oreos-Kraft Foods
Cheerios-General Mills
3M-3M Minnesota Mining and Manufacturing
Volvo Xc90-AB Volvo
CLK1-Amtsgericht München Registergericht
BMW-Amtsgericht München Registergericht
2 Occasions, by Babyface
Please, Baby, Please, by Spike Lee
The Going to Bed Book, by Sandra Boynton
Diaper Genie-Playtex and Energizer Personal Care, LLC
Lightening McQueen-Disney
AMI-Association of Montessori Internationale
Benadryl-McNeil-PPC Inc
iPod-Apple Inc.
Cub-SUPERVALU INC
Impala-General Motors
Melaleuca -The Wellness Company
Amway-Amway
Cutco-CUTCO Cutlery and Vector Marketing
Herbalife-Herbalife International of America, Inc.
Xango-DBC, LLC
Avon-Avon, Products Inc
Elmo-Sesame Workshop
5 Senses, by Jeremiah
Donkey Kong-Nintendo
Scarlett O'hara-Character developed by Margaret Mitchell
Dr. Pepper-Dr. Pepper/Seven Up, Inc
Sex in the City-Home Box Office, Inc
The Big Bang Theory-CBS Interactive
Love and Basketball-40 Acres & A Mule Filmworks
Walgreens-Walgreens Co.

The Fellowship of the Ring, by J. R. R. Toliken
Hush Hush, by Becca Fitzpatrick
The Lightning Thief, by Rick Riordan
Life, the Truth, and Being Free, by Steve Maraboli

Chapter One

Gabbie heard the sound of plastic packages falling in the row behind her. A frustrated groan started to escalate, which peaked her interest. Curiosity, being her downfall every time, made her wander into the next aisle to see a frustrated guy juggling diapers, as a small child, no more than three, used the dropped bundles as building blocks.

Normally she let the chips fall where they may, but this young guy was obviously not a father—or if he was, he was in way over his head. He looked the same age as her with his shoulder length dreads pulled back with a binder, and thick-framed dark glasses. With his striking light caramel color skin and a goatee that was starting to turn into a beard, the man stood at least six-two. What seemed to catch Gabbie's attention the most was his firm build under a University of North Dakota T-shirt and sweatpants.

Gabbie bit at her bottom lip thinking, *if he looks this hot in couch potato clothes, what will he look like dressed up?*

Or better yet, undressed.

The little boy at his feet came up to his knee, with round cheeks and was a little darker than he was. The boy had a slight Afro and, when he looked up at her, she saw the deepest mahogany eyes she'd seen in her

1

life.

The man's frustration grew; he tossed a package of Pampers toward her and she caught it with one hand. *Thank goodness for all those years behind the plate in softball*, she thought.

"You know the no-shopping-cart-theory doesn't work when you have a toddler."

"Huh," he replied absently, "I didn't see you there," he apologized.

"You've obviously never worked in retail and had to clean this crap up." Gabbie bent down on one knee in front of the little boy. "Hey you, what's your name?"

"We're fine, really," the man said right as the little boy cleared the bottom shelf of its merchandise. "Charlie, no," he yelped.

"Charlie, huh? You made a mess, Charlie, and you need to help me clean it up. What if someone did that with your toys?"

Charlie's big eyes, with the longest soft lashes she'd ever seen, looked at her trying to get out of the work. Gabbie scrunched her face in disapproval and Charlie started to put the diapers back on the shelf with his chubby hands, one bundle at a time. Gabbie placed a few on the shelf, but let Charlie do most of the work since he'd made the mess.

"How'd you do that?" the flustered man asked.

"He's a good boy. He's just testing your limits. Uncle? Or does his mom take him shopping?" Gabbie fished for information. God she hoped he wasn't married.

"He's my...I don't know...I'm his guardian."

"That sounds ominous," she replied.

Gabbie restocked the last bundle on the shelf then picked up Charlie, placed him in her virtually empty cart, and buckled him in. Charlie protested at first, but one raised eyebrow from Gabbie stopped him cold. She then grabbed size four Huggies and tossed them in the basket.

"What else do you need, Guardian?"

"I don't even know. Look, he's my brother. My parents were killed in a car wreck two weeks ago. I had one diaper left and..." The man shook his head in despair.

"I'm so sorry. I work with kids every day. Hey, at least he's a boy and not a girl. You'd have to deal with hair and all that stuff."

"Girl? Oh shit, Claire." The man ran frantically up and down the

2

aisles crying out her name.

Gabbie frequented this Walgreens more than she wanted to admit. Something about the crappy As-Seen-On-TV aisle drew her in every time. She headed straight towards the toys and found a little girl that looked the same age as Charlie with definite dad hair pulled up into two lopsided ponytails. She sat with a smashed open package of *Oreos* as her chubby fingers thumbed through a picture book.

"You must be Claire," Gabbie said as she looked at the little girl with chocolate crumbs around her mouth. True to two-year-old form she smiled at Gabbie and held a half-eaten cookie up for her. "Thank you, but you can keep it."

"Oh my god, Claire you can't run off like that," the man said as he tore down the aisle and picked her up, to which she squealed in protest. "Come on lil' bit."

"Claire, be nice to your brother," Gabbie said in a calm voice.

To that, Claire looked at Charlie and passed him the half-eaten cookie, which he took with gusto.

"Thank you for finding her," the man said, dropping the remains of the cookie package in the basket. "You must be ready to call DHS on me."

"No, not yet. I don't even know your name."

"I'm sorry, Case, Case Thomas," he said, hugging Claire closer to his chest and extending his right hand, which Gabbie shook. His hand was soft, but had worn calluses.

"Gabbie Vaulst. You know what, how about a few happy meals on me. There's a McDonalds with a Playland about three blocks from here."

"No, you've done enough."

"I insist, Guardian, and we need to get you some diapers too I suspect," she said to Claire.

"Right, but teach me how to choose what kind?"

"That's simple," she said, pushing back to the baby aisle with Case right on her hip. "First, don't get your diapers in a drug store; they don't have big enough packages. Boys get racecars or sports equipment. Girls tend to have princesses or little animals on them. Other than that look at the weight and figure out if they've out grown the last size you got."

"You have kids."

"Me? No. I run a daycare with my friends. As for size, well you gotta know their weight, but I'm pretty good at that since I'm always lifting kids. You know they're pretty quiet. How old are they?"

"They turned two last Christmas and no they're not quiet, are you, Double Trouble?" Case teased as he nuzzled against Claire's ear. Gabbie was touched.

Charlie blew some spit bubbles at them and Claire giggled at her brother. When Gabbie picked up a package of diapers for Claire, she fell backwards in Case's left arm, as she squealed, "No baby."

"Wait, were you guys getting potty trained?" she asked the kids. "You go to the potty?"

Charlie smiled and clapped his now chocolate crumb covered hands. "Potty, potty oooosss…"

"Diapers are for nigh-nigh only. You two are a big boy and girl aren't you?" Gabbie smiled at the two cherub-faced kids who both seemed delighted a stranger could tell how big they were.

"I have to potty train them now," Case said with utter fear running across his face.

"It looks like they were in the middle of training. You might want some *Cheerios* for Charlie."

"Why?"

"'Cause boys like something to shoot at." She smiled at Case and added two packages of pull-ups to the cart.

"You know, I really could use a Happy Meal," Case said, then sighed. "I may be dumb, but I ain't stupid." His eyes locked on hers and she caught her breath. "You may save me from myself."

* * * *

At McDonalds, Gabbie laid out the food for the two toddlers after securing them in booster seats. Case looked as if she had performed a minor miracle. After cutting up their chicken nuggets, Gabbie looked at Case and smiled.

"It'll get easier. I'm sorry about your parents. You don't have any other siblings do you?"

"No, we're all oopses. I was the prom conception and they were what happened after my parents spent about ten years in failed infertility treatments. I was a freshman at UND when my mom got pregnant. So I don't really know them. I thought about transferring down here when they were born, but I was on scholarship and if I could secure a spot on a team, I'd have had to red shirt a year."

"What did ya play?"

"Basketball. I just came home at Christmas because I was interning at 3M. No, I am interning at 3M," Case corrected himself. "I've got six weeks left in the semester. I'm on a small leave, but I gotta go back soon or I won't be able to graduate in May."

"How long has it been?"

"Two weeks."

"Oh right, you said that. They're still alive. You must be doing something right," Gabbie said, looking at the twins.

Gabbie winced when she realized she just commented about life and death.

"I can't even get through the estate or probate or whatever because these two don't give me a second. I don't want to give them up…"

"Then don't," Gabbie cut him off.

"They need a mother and a father and someone who isn't trying to finish their senior year."

"You've got six weeks left in college. They need someone for life. Look at them. They got your nose and your eyes," Gabbie said as she looked across the table at Case.

Behind his rectangular frames, an amazing set of dark mahogany eyes were framed in the same soft lashes as his little brother. Exhaustion encompassed Case's whole being, yet Gabbie couldn't help but be turned on by the relaxed, gentle tone his deep voice had finally settled into.

"You'll be fine. Give 'em a few more weeks. I promise it'll get better."

Gabbie reached her hand across the table and felt the warmth of his hand under hers. For a moment, their eyes caught and Gabbie could feel a rush surging through her body. She quickly pulled her hand back, from fear of the connection that might have only been one sided.

Case quickly looked at the kids and started to wipe up the ketchup that was being turned into a finger painting project.

"Guys, please, one second of peace."

"No Ace," Charlie said to his big brother.

"No Ace," Claire repeated. "Arlie may mess."

"That is true, Claire," Gabbie said stopping Case from cleaning. "Charlie should help with the mess."

To that, Charlie's bottom lip popped out as he grumbled at Gabbie. "They're too little to understand."

"Now that, you have wrong. They are in the stage of learning proper behavior. And Charlie made a mess, so Charlie should clean it up, with a little help from Gabbie, Claire and Case. Right, Charlie?"

"Yup, Ace, Care and Bee."

"So that's why you talk to them like adults?"

"I'm not having deep discussions about the state of the world, just the state of their world. You talk baby talk, you'll get babies. You don't treat them as equals, but you also don't treat them as imbeciles." She turned back to the kids. "Either way, Charlie and Claire, if you want to go in the tubes this has to be cleaned up first."

Case was too tall to go into the Playland, but Gabbie crawled through the tubes and went down the slides. When she was at the top of the play structure, she looked down and caught Case looking at her. At first, she thought he had been looking for the kids, until she noticed the kids were on their way down the slide, but he kept staring at her.

* * * *

Case left the garage door open so Gabbie could follow him. She had surprised him with her sweet selflessness. He had felt so alone until that evening. His parents had always been there for him when he needed them. Now his life had been divided into before and after his parents' death.

Before, there was guilt built up inside him from the jealousy he'd felt when the twins were born. Having always wanted siblings growing up, he didn't understand his feelings at first. The devotion his parents had shown to him over the years had him trying to prove his independence. The second his parents' attention went to the helpless Charlie and Claire, he reverted and felt that he needed his parents more than ever. He started calling all hours, until his mother finally told him he was grown now and she'll always love him but right now the twins needed her.

The anger he felt from not having his parents traveling the nation to watch him play ball made him stop calling. Then when he got his internship, he found an apartment only a few miles from their house in Woodbury, Minnesota and never even called to tell them he was in town.

After, when he got the phone call from a secretary in the emergency room trying to locate him, he felt a loss in his chest he thought he would never recover from.

As he saw the little pudgy faces of his brother and sister in the care of a babysitter sitting on the couch, he broke down and cried.

"I'll get Charlie if you get Claire," Gabbie offered as she opened the passenger side door of his parents' silver Volvo Xc90.

Case had been glad his parents had paid off the car last year so he didn't have to try to squeeze the kids into the back seat of his CLK1 he got as a graduation gift. Two doors seemed impractical now even though he really missed his old Mercedes parked in the other stall of the garage, left empty since his father's BMW was totaled.

As they entered the house, Case noticed Gabbie had a permanent sparkle in her cool gray eyes surrounded by black eyelashes. Her jet-black hair had been pulled back into a ponytail, except a few strands that outlined the right side of her face. It was all he could do to hold back. He wanted to brush the loose strands back, feel the soft skin of her cheek and press his lips against hers. When he looked at Gabbie all sorts of things triggered in his mind. It seemed as if a lifetime had passed since he last thought about a woman.

He could tell she was one of those girls that wore her clothes a size or two too big because some asshole had told her that her body wasn't shaped right. Case could make out the curves of a woman underneath the layers of protection she wore, and stripped away the layers in his mind.

Gabbie held Charlie in her arms and turned toward him.

"Where's your bathtub?"

A jolt shot straight to his hips and he stepped closer to her. The old Case came rushing forward in the pursuit of a woman he had come to desire. Then Claire, whose favorite time was bath time, knocked him back to reality.

"Baf, baf, baf," she screeched and wiggled to get down his body to the floor and took off to the bathroom.

"I take it she likes bath time?" Gabbie asked with the most brilliant smile.

"That'd be an understatement. Would you be willing to play with Charlie while I give her, her bath?"

"You don't bathe them together?"

"He's a boy, she's a girl."

"And they're two not twelve. Don't make more work for yourself."

Case felt like Gabbie had just smacked him upside his head with a duh. The past week he dreaded bath time, with Claire drenching him as she splashed around as if she was the female Michael Phelps. All the while, Charlie was jumping on his back wanting a ride. Then he tried to put Charlie in the water and he might as well have had a Great Dane the way Charlie thrashed.

"You said at dinner you had papers to sign, but couldn't find a minute in the day. I'll take care of bath time and get them ready for bed. You'll have about a half hour, forty-five minutes."

Just the thought of a half hour without having to entertain or stop the twins from killing themselves rushed adrenaline through Case, as if he had been set free. He didn't know why this woman had taken pity on him and he didn't know how he could repay her.

Gabbie kept the twins occupied while Case found the manila envelope his parents' attorney had given him. With the Wolves game playing in the background, he dumped the papers on the table. Inside had been life insurance papers he needed to file—also, the trust funds his parents had set up for him and the twins, of which he was the executor of until they hit eighteen. It was supposed to help him pay for living expenses for both of them.

Finally, he retrieved the guardianship papers. He had to decide if he was going to adopt his brother and sister and become their father, stay their legal guardian, or sign away all rights to them. He was just starting out and couldn't even find diapers for them without his hand being held. How could he take on the responsibility of two lives when he could barely manage his?

At least the house was paid for and after he signed three more lines, it would be his to raise the kids in or sell. He finished signing all the financial papers and, placing the three custody choices in front of him, bent his head in prayer.

Why couldn't he just have a simple sign telling him what to do?

Behind him, he heard little patters on the floor and Charlie crawled up on his right side and Claire on his left. They were in their footy pajamas smelling of Johnson and Johnson with their tight, curly, black hair still damp from the bath.

"Nigh nigh, Ace," they both said giving him a kiss on each cheek.

"Nigh nigh, monsters," he said holding their warm, little bodies close to him. They both had their chubby arms wrapped around his neck and, for the first time since his parents had died, something felt right.

"Okay, little ones," he heard Gabbie say. "I got *Please, Baby, Please,* so let's get going before I'm too tired to read to you."

Case turned around to see Gabbie. Her T-shirt and sweatpants had splatters of water on them, but she wasn't soaked like he usually was after a bath, and her hair still had some bubbles on the side he assumed came from Claire. As the kitchen light cut across her face he couldn't imagine a more beautiful woman. Her hair was disheveled and she looked like she'd just finished a step class at the gym, but the pink flush in her cheeks was enough to make him wonder what had changed in just thirty minutes.

Charlie and Claire climbed down and he heard them patter away down to Gabbie's open hands. With one on each side, they walked peacefully to their room and the only thing Case could remember was Gabbie's ass as she walked away.

What the hell was the matter with him?

* * * *

After tucking in the babies, Gabbie took in the room. Dirty clothes littered the floor around the overflowed hamper. She was sure the *Diaper Genie* was filled to capacity—that is if Case had figured out how to use it. The only clear spots were the two toddler beds on either side of the room.

She couldn't imagine how hard it must be on Case. Not only to lose your parents, but then to become a parent to two beautiful children. Contrary to what he must think, Charlie and Claire loved him; they were just confused about where their mommy and daddy were.

"Ace funny," Claire had giggled in the tub.

Gabbie was sure if their vocabulary was more developed she could have heard all about the misadventures of Case and the kids. Shaking her head, she headed back to the living room to see Case with his head buried in his hands and his elbows rested on his knees. In front of him were three sets of documents.

"Did you figure out all the paperwork you needed to?" Gabbie asked and broke his concentration.

"Most of it." He sighed and lay back on the couch. "They're asleep? You were only gone fifteen minutes."

"I know." Gabbie smiled, loving his amazement at her ability with his…well she guessed they were his kids now.

She curled a leg underneath her and sat at the edge of the light green microfiber couch. Case looked spent. Dark circles were under his eyes and she could see the worry across his forehead.

"You're phenomenal. It takes me two hours to get them to bed."

"You want to know a secret?"

"I need to if I'm going to survive."

"I have to touch you to show you. Is that okay?"

Case swallowed hard and seemed uncomfortable. Gabbie pulled back. She hadn't been helping him because he was sexy as hell and she wanted to sleep with him. Okay, that had crossed her mind about twenty million times since they met. When the twins crawled on his lap to kiss him good night she'd had heat rush straight to her hips. The three of them seemed on the edge of a cliff and she couldn't help her desire to save them.

"I guess," he finally replied while shifting his hips.

"Lay back," she said as she moved to sit right next to him.

Lightly, she removed his glasses and set them on the coffee table by the paperwork. Lowering her voice, she explained as her finger lightly stroked his eyebrows.

"I don't know why this works, but all you need to do is run your fingers over their eyebrows like this…"

Case mumbled something and she soon realized that it wasn't just babies this trick worked on. A few more soothing strokes with her finger and Case's face completely relaxed. His breathing slowed and he was out.

Gabbie got up, found a navy blue blanket on a quilt rack by the TV and placed it over Case. Then she went into the kitchen which was disaster area number one hundred and two. Case needed a fresh start in the morning. Gabbie looked at the clock on the microwave and saw it was only nine o'clock. She decided to get a load or two of laundry going while she cleaned the kitchen.

She started the dishwasher, and then hand washed the last of the dishes and put them away. Case's parents had to have been rich, which was impressive considering he was an "oops" from high school. She could understand an "oops" from college, but to be able to make it to a house with a gourmet kitchen in Woodbury from two high school sweethearts showed her the strength of character Case must have been brought up in.

The kitchen had granite countertops and an island that was about the size of her whole kitchen. Cherry wood cabinets went almost all the way to what had to be at least ten-foot ceilings. All the appliances were stainless steel. On the fridge were random snapshots of Case's parents with him at a bar-b-que when he must have been in high school and then in the hospital with Charlie and Claire.

They all had their father's dark eyes and their mother's button nose. Emergency numbers were on the fridge as well as a magnet from The Caring Tree, an upscale daycare center that she was sure expected to be paid in advance—probably seven hundred dollars at least every week for twins. She found six other flyers around the kitchen, all of them with smiling children and a fee schedule she knew as a college student Case couldn't afford.

He must have an inheritance…or was that what he was filling out all evening? The papers must be for all the red tape to release the money needed to take care of his siblings. Gabbie redid her ponytail and decided to pick up the toys from around the house and put them away, then leave. She'd given him a good start and that would have to be enough. The thought of her touch seemed to send a fear shot through him and she could get the hint.

Michel Prince

* * * *

A buzz woke Case and he looked for Gabbie. It was still dark outside, so he turned on the table lamp and found his glasses. As he refocused his eyes, he saw the living room that had been filled with trucks, dolls and a dozen other toys scattered to the wind was now clean. All the toys had been put into the baskets on either side of the entertainment center.

A buzz went off again, so he followed the sound coming from the kitchen. In the utility room he saw the dryer rotating the drum, then stopping to buzz again. On top of the dryer had to be three loads of clean and folded laundry. The dryer rotated one more time then stopped.

Gabbie had washed clothes, picked up the living room and could it be possible... he dared to dream as he entered the now clean kitchen. On the empty counter of the island he saw a note.

> *Case,*
> *Thought you could use a fresh start now that you know how to get the kids to sleep. I wish you the best of luck in the future. Claire and Charlie are lucky to have you as their guardian. They really do love you. You should have heard them in the bath...Ace this and Ace that.*
> *Anyway. I'm not sure if you've found a daycare yet, but here's my card. I know I have space in my toddler room and you can pay me when the probate is through. Feel free to drop them off any time after six am. Just fill out the admission sheets to the best of your ability, and bring two packages of pull-ups. Remember Lighting McQueen for Charlie and the three princesses for Claire.*
> *Best of luck,*
> *Gabbie*

Case fingered the card with its pink blocks along the side. *Gabbie Vaulst, Educational Director.* She sure had taught him a ton in a few hours. He'd actually be able to go to work tomorrow.

He remembered the story she told him over dinner of how she became a business owner at eighteen. One of her friends, Mary, had become pregnant. She had been on a softball team with Mary, Mandy and Sarah since they were little. Even though others came and went from the sport, the four of them always made the team.

Gabbie was the catcher, which explained her quick hands with the diapers and her deliciously thick thighs and ass. Case shook his head and tried to refocus more on what Gabbie had said, and less on the way he wanted to dig his fingers into her hips.

Mary was the pitcher, Sarah was first base, and Mandy was third. They had a rhythm between them, having always had to count on each other. When Mary got pregnant, they all came together and turned down the scholarships they had earned to start a business and help her.

Case had teammates he'd been close with over the years, but he never thought he'd give up college to help one of them out. But then again, he was giving up graduate school to raise his brother and sister.

When kids are involved, all bets are off.

For some reason, Gabbie's paperwork didn't seem like a chore. Maybe it was because she somehow knew the kids' pediatrician and dentist and all he had to do was fill out their birthdays and his contact info.

With how overwhelmed he'd been feeling, just the thought she was around was enough to clear the gray skies that seemed to loom over him. With a plan for tomorrow, Case took a shower, but found he kept washing one area. *Jesus*, he thought, *a woman helps me for a few hours and all I can think about was how soft her neck would feel against my lips.* Or the way she would feel sliding over his hips. Her tight T-shirt held snug to her chest and she seemed to have a small pooch in the front, but she wasn't fat. She was the way he liked his woman, thick and defined.

His hand started to increase his stroke speed and right as he remembered Gabbie's smile his sack clenched and a rush shot out of him, clearing his mind. He wanted her, but he had to think about why before he pursued her. If it was just because of the twins, that wouldn't be fair to anyone involved. And now he couldn't just date—he was a father and Claire and Charlie needed stability.

13

Michel Prince

Toweling off, he was content in the fact that he'd at least have the idea of Gabbie. His last girlfriend had turned him off women for the last few months. Somehow having something besides the kids to focus on seemed to lighten him and help him see beyond the next few minutes. Once again, he could see the future and for some unknown reason there wasn't a second that didn't include Gabbie smiling at him.

Chapter Two

"These words reveal the child's inner needs; 'Help me to do it alone'."
                                        —Maria Montessori

The doorbell rang at the Growing Strong Daycare center in Maplewood, a suburb of St. Paul, that Gabbie was part owner of. Inside she was hoping it was Case and not some random parent looking to check out the facility. She didn't want to sprint to the front door to make it obvious, but unfortunately Mandy beat her to the door.

Mandy had on a tight yellow T-shirt and khaki colored skinny jeans. Her dish-water blond hair was cut in a cute little bob with longer hair in the front and the back layered all the way down to a clean shave at the base of her neck.

"Can I help you?" Mandy asked, but Gabbie, seeing that it was in fact Case and company, decided to take control.

"I've got this, Mandy. These are the Thomas' and they're starting here today."

"Hi Gabbie." Case's deep voice carried straight to her heart.

Gabbie had to hold her hands together to stop from shaking. Today he was in a pressed French blue shirt with white accented cuffs and collar, and a dark charcoal gray tie. He had a kid on each hip and the diaper bags slung over his shoulder.

Case's goatee had been trimmed tight and outlined his full dark lips. He wasn't wearing his glasses and Gabbie didn't know how to react with his mahogany eyes no longer locked behind a set of frames. But what got her going the most was when he walked in the door he still looked petrified until he saw her. The relief that washed over his face as he saw her made her feel like she was the only woman he ever wanted to see.

"Pant much?" Mandy murmured as she passed. "Dads are off limits."

"He's a guardian," Gabbie snapped back. "And it's married dads that are off limits…why did we start that policy again?"

"I miss the Kincaids," Mandy passively mused.

Mandy was one of Gabbie's best friends, even if she made bad choices as often as Joan Rivers went in for a surgical procedure.

As soon as Charlie and Claire were set down, they took off to Gabbie who dropped to one knee to accept their hugs.

"Bee…bee…" they sang in unison each giving her a good squeeze.

"Ace finded my pin kirt," Claire said, spinning in a circle with a dark green dress that flew up showing her tights that Gabbie didn't want to tell Case were on backwards.

"You look beautiful today. And Charlie, that's a pretty cool coat you have on today." Charlie smiled then zerberted Gabbie's cheek. "Well let's show you where you guys get to hang out with me and my friends while Case has to go to work," Gabbie said with a disgusted look on her face.

The kids giggled and followed her into the toddler room. There were already four kids in the room and they came running over to meet the strangers. Alice was the oldest. In a few months she'd be moved to the next room, but she was very type A and went straight for Claire.

"I'm Alice," she said, clear as day. The baby talk she had been using when she started six months ago was long gone. She was a big girl now. "Come play with me. What's your name?"

Gabbie knew there would be about seven thousand questions from Alice today. She was happy that at least for today, it wouldn't be her having to deal with them. In the corner was Taylor. He was shy and perfect for Charlie. Walking Charlie over to Taylor, Gabbie made introductions then returned to Case since Sarah was in the room monitoring the kids.

"Let's get your paperwork in order, Case," Gabbie said, and placed the diaper bags on the table for Sarah to set up boxes.

Gabbie's hand brushed against the back of Case's. They both stopped and looked at each other. He smiled at her. Maybe there was a chance, but she tried to not read too much into the gesture.

In Gabbie's office, she closed the glass door so they could at least speak in privacy. Case passed her the forms she'd left for him and she started entering the information in their database.

"I can't thank you enough for what you did for me last night."

"It was nothing. You were just a little behind on things. With kids, that happens."

"You did a lot. It was the first goodnight sleep I'd had in the last two weeks."

Gabbie looked up at him and saw the dark circles were gone and he looked refreshed.

"Can't help the Thomases have a weak spot. So, are you going to keep them?"

"Yeah, I just don't know if I should be their father or…"

"Ace?"

He smiled at her

"It seems weird someone would call me daddy."

Gabbie had an unnatural reaction to the way he said daddy. A vision flashed through her mind of him wiping off her desk and coming from behind her. As he thrust himself inside her, he begged her to call him daddy. He must have seen something on her face because he smiled wide.

"What's the difference between adoption and guardianship?" Gabbie asked to get back on track.

He leaned on the edge of her desk. "You mean besides the daddy part?"

Gabbie sat back in her chair and tried to regain her composure.

"Guardianship is temporary. I'd be like a foster parent. I just don't want them to forget my mom and dad. But they could be listed as available for adoption too."

"Just because the paper work says you're their father doesn't mean you can't still be Ace. You probably need to get to work and I'm sure it's time for my first lesson."

"I suppose I should have asked you what you teach the kids here."

"I told you about me and my friends choosing this over college, right? After a year or so, we learned about Montessori teaching philosophies and decided we wanted to turn this into a school someday. There's only a few training centers in the country and we're lucky enough to have one in the Twin Cities. We're all at different levels so we don't all get stuck interning at the same time. I'm in my second year of the training. Since it's at night, because most people are teachers already, it works perfect."

"And you still have time to help lost men in drug stores."

"I troll for clients there. Anyway, we do lesson plans similar to the Montessori method. It empowers the children to become independent—at least at the Children's house age. We don't have many older children, but luckily I'm studying newborns to five year olds. If they were older I might not have been able to help you as much."

"So you gonna make the little monsters self-sufficient."

"No, but they'll be able to learn the importance of maintaining their own space, which should help you."

Case looked at his watch and sighed. "I've got to get going. I get done around five."

"We're open until six. Can you make it back by then?"

Case nodded and stood up. Gabbie couldn't help but take in his lean, firm body that was almost a foot taller than her. Sitting down she hadn't noticed how much he filled the room up.

"I'm really glad you brought them in."

"I forgot. How much is this going to cost?"

"Right now, nothing. But we charge one fifty a week for the first kid and a hundred for the second. Also, we ask you provide groceries for the room once every..." Gabbie tried to remember how many were now in the toddler room. "It'd be every six weeks I think since they're two. It usually costs about two hundred dollars."

"Once I get access to their trust, I can have a check drawn directly from the account."

"I trust you, Case," Gabbie said, extending her hand. Case surrounded her hand with his warm fingers and they seemed to stand together longer than either was comfortable with.

They both coughed out of nerves and Case seemed to rush for the door. Gabbie slumped in her chair. Every part of her was tingling and she needed to get back to the task at hand—a sand writing lesson in the four and five-year-old room.

"He's gorgeous," Mandy said, sliding into the chair Case had been sitting in.

"Aren't you in the infant room today?"

"We're training in that new girl we hired. So spill."

"Nothing to spill," Gabbie said, clicking her pen shut and pushing up from her desk. "He needed daycare so he could finish his internship."

"And the baby momma?"

"His parents were killed in a car wreck. Charlie and Claire are his brother and sister. His mom was a stay at home mother so they didn't have daycare. He'd been looking at all the daycares in his area and decided there was no way he could afford any of them right now."

"So he's not the babies' daddy?"

"No, he's a senior in college who just had his world turned upside down."

"Oh…"

"You sound disappointed."

"I just don't know how to deal with that."

"Don't. He's off limits for the foreseeable future."

"You want him."

"I want him to heal. He just lost his parents."

Mandy followed Gabbie out of the office teasing all the way.

"You want him, you want him. Gabbie wants a little sexual chocolate—"

"Hi, girls." Mrs. Stevens stopped them with her cold prosecuting attorney stare and Gabbie just wanted to die.

"Hi, Sadie," Gabbie said after she recovered. "Let's get your stuff in the cubbies. I apologize for Ms. Mandy."

"We've been here for two years. We're used to Amanda. Just keep it for nap time, girls," Mrs. Stevens said as she walked out the door.

"Yes, ma'am," Mandy replied and scuttled off to the infant room as if she had been scolded by the principal.

Gabbie spent the rest of the day trying to forget about Case as she taught her lessons, but in the toddler room she had two sets of dark mahogany eyes that made it impossible.

* * * *

Case got to work with five minutes to spare. Not having to rush, he stopped by the break room to grab a pop before he went into the lab. That turned out to be a mistake. Everyone seemed to be there. The condolences and I'm-so-sorry-for-your-losses had him on edge. He grieved in silence, not with people and their placating comments. Case knew they meant well, but they might as well have covered him in paper cuts and poured pure lemonade over him.

Then to top it off, the cougar approached—or the one who thought she was a cougar. It's not that Case didn't like someone a little older now and then, but this crazy woman was a few awkward gropes away from a sexual harassment suit. She was a secretary in the next department and had been using his area's break room since three days after he started.

"Hello Case, we missed you," Tanya gushed as the overly flowered perfume assaulted his every sense.

He could taste it in the back of his throat and for the first time since he had got there, she'd pissed him off. Case had been savoring the fresh clean smell that lingered on his hand from Gabbie.

With Tanya's thick blond hair covering her left eye he was glad he only had to see half of her made up face. To amuse himself he'd calculate the chemical formulas of her hairspray, make-up, and perfume together to make sure she hadn't accidentally created deadly mustard gas. The smell that wafted off her was similar.

"Good morning," he said, tucking his tie into the center of his shirt so it wouldn't be damaged in the lab. He side-stepped her, but she stepped in front of him and chuckled as if it was an accident.

"How those babies?" Tanya had a twang to her voice that could grate cheese. "You need any help with them?"

Tanya had five kids…maybe. He'd seen her desk and it seemed like that many. All he knew was one of them was only two years younger than him. He thanked God Gabbie had been in the store last night and not Tanya, or he might have actually taken her up on her offers.

"I'm good. Found a nice daycare for them. A friend's helping me out."

"You know those daycares can't take the place of a good momma," she growled, taking a step towards him with her fake nails grasping for his tie. His escape was foiled because he backed into the counter.

"I need to talk to my supervisor and get checked in," Case said, scooting past and boxing out to get past her.

Rushing to the lab, he checked in with his boss and got back to work. His co-workers were glad he was back—if for no other reason than they had been having to watch the changes on his experiment as well as their own. He had one of ten variables off of an original polymer. Currently he and Traun were the ones that had cracked the initial code.

Somehow Case was supposed to increase the water solubility and make the product safe enough to be used on skin. He was supposed to focus on this breathable liquid band aid with antibiotic disbursement, but all during the day Case was worried about the twins. He believed Gabbie would protect them, but they had never really been around other kids without his mom or dad.

Case tried sketching out the chemical formula in an effort to distract himself. Instead, on the side of the page, he started sketching out Gabbie's eyes.

"I don't think I know that formula…" Traun joked as he poked his head in his cubical. "It looks like chemistry's involved though."

"Yeah, maybe," Case admitted, then stretched, taking in Traun's plain white shirt with blue tie that he seemed to wear every day. "Is there something you needed?"

Traun was short and stocky in the Hmong tradition. Second generation though, with no trace of an accent, and with respect for the ancient ways, but not controlled by them.

"Mr. Clarkson wants to team us all up. They have two positions open that we are in competition for. I figured we could team up and roll over the others. I know my fiancée would love for me to have a stable job when I graduate."

"I could use that too," Case admitted, "especially now. Hey, could you help me with a problem?"

"Well, I know you're going to need at least two more carbon atoms to make that work," Traun suggested.

"Not formulary…and I'm thinking of adding a nitrogen to accelerate the sealing process. There's a secretary over in accounting that keeps coming on to me."

"One or two? Nitrogen, not secretaries."

"Won't two make it unstable?"

"It isn't in cyanoacrylate, that they had in spray form during Vietnam. We could work it out in the lab after lunch. Let me guess…Tanya?"

"Yes, you too?"

"No, she just seems like the type. My girl is at William and Mary taking law classes. I'll try to catch her at lunch."

At lunch Case called the daycare center and talked to Gabbie. She assured him both kids were doing fine, but until he saw them he wouldn't be comfortable. Maybe he *was* a father. Losing Claire last night had his heart pounding as every bad news story ran through his head. He was so sure he'd lost her forever.

Case spent the afternoon in the lab with Traun as they avoided an explosion, but still had fun trying to knock out issues. Case was enjoying using his brain for something other than trying to figure out the ramblings of his brother and sister. Around three o'clock he took a break when his phone rang and his heart raced. It was daycare.

"This is Case."

"First inhale," Gabbie ordered.

"Why?" Case asked, not responding to her order.

"Because I can hear your heart beating over the phone and you're about to throw up."

Case breathed in deep then exhaled. "Happy now?"

"Just letting you know that kids are doing fine…"

"But."

"I didn't say but."

"You didn't need to. What happened?"

"Claire fell on the playground and has a fat lip."

"What!" he snapped. "I'll be right there."

"No, you won't."

22

"Excuse me."

"Case, they're going to fall down. They're going to get hurt, especially when they go mach one across the playground for a plastic bat because they swore they heard the word bath."

Case could only imagine his sister knocking down other kids to be the first one in the tub.

"She didn't strip while she was running, did she?"

"Yea…um…the bigger issue is your sister is allergic to some type of berry."

"Allergic…I didn't know…"

"We give kids popsicles when they bump their lips or lose a tooth…"

"What kind of death chamber did you talk me into putting my kids?"

"Case—"

"No. Don't Case me. They're all I got left in the world."

"Then you should learn their allergies. As I said, she's allergic to a berry. I don't know which one because it was a mixed berry popsicle. But she needs to be evaluated by Dr. Conrad sooner rather than later so we know what to keep away from her and more importantly if we need more than Benadryl."

"Gabbie, it won't be an issue because this will be her last day there."

"I'm sorry you feel that way, but Case…the only reason this was even an issue was because you have children you need to learn about."

He hated that she was right. And that he'd snapped on her.

"I called because I dispensed Benadryl without your permission. It was enough to stop her wheezing and she's doing fine now, but you're going to need to see if you can get a follow up visit tonight with her doctor."

"I don't even know who that is," he said, sighing and dropping his head in shame.

He covered his eyes with his hand as he rested his elbow on the table.

"Gabbie…" His voice caught; that was twice in less than twenty-four hours he could have lost Claire. It was one thing to lose control of his life, but he couldn't do that to his innocent brother and sister. "Help me."

"You still hate me and think I torture children in my spare time?"

"No," he said swallowing hard.

"This one time, I'll make the appointment. When I call you back, you better do whatever you can to get here in time to get her there."

"I will… Gabbie, how did you know who their doctor was?"

"It was on the fridge. I'll call you back in the next half hour with a time. And Case…"

"Yes?" he replied, afraid of what she'd say next.

"Charlie used the bathroom by himself."

Case snorted. "Why would you tell me that?"

"Because he said that you hit more *Cheerios* than him this morning. Way to go, dad."

* * * *

When Case came through the door, he bee-lined for the toddler room.

"In here, Case," Gabbie called from the infant room. "We only have three kids left so we put them all in the same room. Did you have a good day at work?" Gabbie bit her tongue because she almost added *honey* on the end.

Charlie and Claire smothered Case, who had dropped to his knees, with hugs.

"A breakthrough actually," he replied as he looked over Claire's face. "I thought you said she had a fat lip?"

"She could have, but we put ice on it."

"Ace…ouch," Claire dramatically told of her accident. Her big eyes turned to Gabbie as if it still hurt.

"You've had three popsicles. That's enough, little miss. Now you two, do you remember where your coats are?"

"I's do Bee," Charlie said taking off down the hall with Claire a half a step behind him.

"I have one more favor to ask then I promise I won't ask for another thing for at least five minutes," Case said.

"With a promise like that, how could I refuse?" Gabbie said with a smile.

Before Case could ask, Bonnie came in to pick up little Lewis who was fast asleep in his car seat already. Case left to help the twins get ready to go and Gabbie finished locking up the infant room.

"Would you come to the doctor with me? I don't know what to ask and I don't want 'em to die because I'm a moron."

"You're far from a moron...maybe just a little slow," she teased and stepped in closer to him, removing a piece of lint from his shoulder.

A little part of her was praying for a kiss as his fingers wrapped around her loose hair, tucking it behind her ear. Gabbie began to tremble and licked her lips as Case took another step closer to her. Case leaned in when Charlie pulled on his pants.

"Up Ace. Up."

"I just got cock blocked by a two-year-old."

"I wouldn't call it a full-on block."

"You wouldn't?"

"No."

"This isn't one sided?"

"Up...Bee," Claire ordered.

"We need to leave now to get her to the doctor on time."

"Life or death, huh?"

"It could be."

Gabbie bent down to pick up Claire and saw a bulge in Case's pants.

"You need a minute?"

"Yes please."

Flattered at Case's reaction to her, she took Charlie's hand, snagged Case's keys from his finger and walked out to get the kids in the car. Once locked in their car seats, Case came to the car.

"You want to follow in your car?"

"I walked. I live around the corner. Just let me turn on the security system and we're off."

When Gabbie came back outside she could hear Case talking to the kids because Claire's window wasn't closed.

"All I'm saying is cut me a little slack. You know how long it's been since a girl...made me feel good. If I'm close to Gabbie...find a toy."

"Bee's a toy?" Claire asked with her hands turned palm up in confusion. "Bee not a toy?"

"I didn't say Gabbie's a toy, I said… Never mind."

Opening the car door, Gabbie slid in the seat, giggling.

"What?"

"If you can get a two-year-old to understand not to interrupt kissing, you'll be a millionaire."

"You heard that?"

Gabbie crossed over Case and pressed the rear window up, then engaged the window lock. She did this all without looking at the controls. Instead, she kept her eyes locked on Case's.

"I make you feel…good," she teased and Case smiled. "Just good?"

"Very…good."

"Hmmm…" Gabbie let out a sigh then looked down. "Keep the window lock on or they'll find a way to crawl out when you're going sixty miles per hour."

"You're the best teacher…ever," Case said as Gabbie let her hand brush across his hips.

Gabbie sat back in her seat, buckled up and Case took off. A minute into the ride, Case's fingers entwined with Gabbie's and he laid their hands on her thigh. She looked over to him and saw a half smile on his lips. There was definitely something there.

It had been easier than Gabbie thought to get an appointment for Claire, even this late into the afternoon. In the doctor's office, Case sat with his leg bouncing and Gabbie had to calm him down by stroking his thigh. Gabbie asked all the questions she could think of and the doctor was very sympathetic of Case's circumstance. When they left Case had learned about shot schedules, allergies and that Charlie had gotten ear tubes about three months ago. He also left with a prescription for an epi-pen, just in case, because Claire had already had an allergic reaction to blackberries in the past, although it wasn't as bad as what happened at daycare.

Otherwise the twins were adjusting well considering all that had happened over the last month. Heading back home, Case asked if Gabbie would mind helping him get the kids to bed again.

Gabbie had to suppress the thought that she could go to bed with him.

Chapter Three

"Gravitation cannot be held responsible for people falling in love."

—Albert Einstein

Case wasn't sure what was going on between Gabbie and him. All he could think of was his dad telling him he'd seen his mother across the cafeteria and knew he had to have her. But when he talked to her, his world opened up and he went from a free agent to someone anchored and no longer adrift. Case felt settled since Gabbie had caught his errantly thrown diapers.

"You know I can't do this every night until they're eighteen," Gabbie teased.

"I know. I needed you to teach me the bath trick."

"Did you hear that Claire? Case said it's time for a bath."

"Mach one," Case said as Claire took off for the bathroom.

"Does she have another speed?" Gabbie asked.

Claire was trying to undress herself as they walked in the bathroom with Charlie. Gabbie started to fill the tub with the rubber ducky safety spout and added bubbles to the water. Claire, of course, was the first one in with Charlie dragging his feet like they were asking him to dip himself in acid.

Case stood back and let Gabbie show him how she wrangled Charlie in the tub without him turning into a sixties peace marcher. Gabbie was so patient and funny as she told Charlie he couldn't go in the water.

"No. Don't you go in there Charles," she warned and he inched closer. "If I catch you in the bathtub again…" she growled and Charlie laughed as he quickly crawled in before Gabbie could catch him.

"Got you Bee," he chuckled. "I fast."

"Yes, you're too fast for me."

Claire was splashing and Case waited to see how Gabbie kept her shirt so dry last night.

"You're getting wet," he whispered in her ear then realized what he had said. "From the bath."

"Last night I took off my shirt and tucked it away in the linen closet to keep it dry."

Case stripped off his shirt and tossed it in the hall. Gabbie's eyes slid down his muscular frame. Although he hadn't been working out as much as he wanted to lately he still had definition in his abs and biceps. And Gabbie seemed to appreciate that. Her bright red tongue licked at her bottom lip. Then she bit the freshly moistened skin.

"Your turn," he said, right as Claire did a huge splash covering the back of Gabbie's shirt. "I'm going to have to call her my wingman now."

Gabbie took off her soaked shirt and tossed it in the sink. She and Case washed the kids and Gabbie taught him how to wash their hair without the protests he'd been getting. When they were done with the washing, Gabbie told Case to let them play.

"It'll wear them out and make Charlie like bath time as much as Claire."

"I'm starting to love bath time," Case said as his finger traced the strap of Gabbie's bra.

A shiver shot through Gabbie when Case's finger went underneath the strap and his skin touched hers. He moved closer and placed his hand on her back, then slowly lowered her down to the floor and hovered above her lips. Gabbie felt her body warm against his bare, smooth chest pressed against hers.

"Dook Care, Ace and Bee dook dike mama and daddy," Charlie said, laughing.

"He did it again," Case said irritated. "Grab a towel, she's gonna run."

"Huh?" Gabbie asked, still lost in the faint smell of Case's cologne.

"Mama...Ace where mama," Claire started to shriek and Gabbie heard the sloshing of her getting out of the tub as the heat of Case's body disappeared.

"Claire, you can't run around naked," Case said, chasing after Claire with a towel.

"What wrong with Care?" Charlie asked, and Gabbie wasn't sure what to do.

"I guess she's sad about your mommy and daddy," Gabbie said as she started to drain the tub, took Charlie out, and dried him off.

"Ace daddy now," Charlie said simply.

"You understand that?" Gabbie asked, amazed.

"Daddy and mama bump head." Charlie smacked his forehead, and Gabbie now understood him freaking out when Claire got hurt. "Bee you mama now?" he asked with his beautiful mahogany eyes inquisitive, but not pleading.

"No, Charlie, I'm not your mommy now. But Case is your daddy."

"Ace silly daddy."

"Yeah, Case is a silly daddy, but he loves you lots and that's important."

They walked into the twin's room and Gabbie got Charlie ready for bed. Claire and Case were still somewhere in the house. After Charlie went to sleep Gabbie got Claire's pajamas and walked around the house until she heard Claire still crying in a room.

Case was sitting on what must have been their parents' bed in the master bedroom. It was a pine four poster, king size bed with a sage green comforter. Claire was curled up in Case's arms still wrapped in the towel. Her sobs were icicles that shot through Gabbie as each one of Claire's huge tears fell. Case was rocking her telling her that he missed mommy too. He promised to never leave her.

It was strange that Charlie was the introvert that understood the situation and Claire the extrovert was having problems with comprehending mommy and daddy wouldn't be back. Either way, in this situation, Gabbie felt as lost as Case. She crawled on the bed next to them. Claire looked at her with tear soaked cheeks and dark eyes muddied by tears that hadn't escaped yet. Pulling away from Case and crawling on Gabbie's lap, Claire was snuggling against her chest.

"Bee, I's miss mama."

"I bet you do. I wish I'd met her. She seemed really special."

"Mama no here."

"I know."

After dressing Claire, the three of them curled up in the bed and fell asleep.

* * * *

Case woke first that morning with Claire curled into his chest and Gabbie spooning the two of them. He played with Gabbie's hair for a few minutes before she started to stir too.

"It's morning?" she asked as she stretched out. "You think my shirt's dry?"

"I don't know, but these two will be moving soon."

"Right, I'll go get my shirt."

Case caught Gabbie's wrist and pulled her back into bed.

"You know if there wasn't a two-year-old between us..." he growled.

"But she is. And we need to do what's best for them. Charlie asked me if I was his new mommy yesterday."

"He did?" Case asked and released her wrist.

"And I'm not completely sure what's between us...isn't just you being alone and me being available. Either way, you can't have women coming in and out of their lives because they can't understand adult relationships. I don't understand adult relationships."

Case had to admit the thought had crossed his mind, but that didn't mean what they were feeling wasn't real.

"I don't want to be the girl who you found when you were desperate, because I'm not, so the fact that I'm falling hard for you is real. Which means when you're on your feet and leave me because you settled..."

Gabbie pushed off the bed, unable to verbalize the rest.

Were his feelings real or not? The fact he couldn't answer that question immediately scared him. He was sure he wanted to date Gabbie, because she was naturally sexy, not made up with so many fake parts you didn't know where the real person began. And every part of Gabbie was real down to the words from her full pink lips that glistened when her tongue would glide... Case pushed off the bed on that one.

Did he want to sleep with her? Hell yes. But there was more to his desires than carnal cravings and a potential replacement mom; he was certain of it. He needed to prove it to Gabbie, and if being away for a while would do that, he'd distract himself by learning to be a good dad.

* * * *

Gabbie was glad Tuesdays were her day off. It gave her time away from Charlie and Claire, because their eyes were like an innocent Case's. They were attaching to her as if she were a parent and worst yet, she was falling in love with the whole Thomas family.

Case came with too much baggage. Not too much for her to handle, but the kind of baggage that had her questioning his reason for being with her. As much as it killed her to not see Case, she knew she'd always have doubts about their relationship if it was built on desperation.

Gabbie worked typing up a paper while her black and white spotted cat Lucy lay on her forearms, making it almost impossible to type.

"Really Lucy? You couldn't sit next to me with your head on my lap?"

Lucy responded the way Gabbie expected, by turning her blue eyes up to her then yawning and laying her head down on her outstretched paws. To which Gabbie picked her up and tossed her on the floor. With a huff, Lucy walked off and curled up on the heating vent.

"Because I can always throw a blanket around myself so I don't need heat. Thanks Luce, you're a peach," Gabbie said and then dropped her head. "I'm arguing with a cat now. I'm talking to myself. I'm becoming the crazy cat lady."

Gabbie picked up her cell phone and scanned her numbers for Case's, then let her finger hover over the send button. How bad would it be? Being settled for by a hot, smart guy with two kids. She dropped the phone back on the coffee table, then put her feet up and finished working on her paper.

Her little apartment wasn't the homey place that Case's was. It was a simple one bedroom with kitchen that was practically in the living room. Or vice versa depending on how you looked at it. As she put fresh sheets onto her little bed, she thought about how it could never hold Case's height. She shook her head. How long had it been since a man was in her bed? Oh right, never. It was high school the last time she got anything and that wasn't worth the fifty cents the loser paid for a gas station condom.

Why was she even thinking about sex with Case? He'd need a damn dust buster to get through the spider webs, and a tennis racket to knockdown bats that would probably fly out of her if she ever uncrossed her damn legs. God, why did he have to turn her on so much? She eyed the top drawer of her nightstand, then shook her head at the thought. The stupid toy Mandy bought her as a gag gift hadn't hit any spots either. Hell, she probably didn't even have a spot to hit. She looked down at Lucy who rubbed her head against Gabbie's legs.

"You want a brother or sister? Because I think it's just going to be you and me for a long time."

Lucy raised her tail as she walked away from Gabbie's suggestion in disgust. *I'm not even a good cat lady*, Gabbie thought as she spent the rest of the morning cleaning her apartment.

Her phone rang a little after noon with a call from the center.

"Gabbie," Mary Beth snapped before Gabbie could even say hello. "Why do we have two new kids in the toddler room, but I don't even see a check to be brought to the bank? Mandy said something about you doing a favor for a friend. This is a business, not a charity for every stray you find on the side of the road."

Gabbie did have a reputation for helping out people in the past—even going as far as allowing a mother to drop off her kids only when she had interviews and without warning, but Case was different. Yes, he was a gamble, but she knew he could be trusted. Money was just tight right now for him. Getting the point across to Mary Beth wouldn't be easy. She was the financial genius that kept them afloat mostly because she had extra motivation. Little Lukey, her son was, as Case would call him, an oops.

"Are you going to explain this or not?"

"His parents just died. The money to raise the kids is tied up in a trust that his lawyer has to file paperwork on. No freebies, I promise."

"I heard what he looks like. You sure he isn't using you?"

"To save two fifty a week on daycare? No."

"He needs to put something down. We're upside down enough."

"And by upside down we have less than twenty-five k in excess

32

income."

Mary Beth was a genius, but she also tended to overinflate their dire straits. Most of the time, they were at full capacity. That's why they had just hired two new people so they could legally take on more kids. The openings in the toddler room were just dumb luck with kids aging out and infants not aging in for another few weeks.

"How long will it be before I can see some income from this father?"

"Well if he screws me right, never," Gabbie sneered.

"That's not funny."

"Neither is your attitude. He'll get us the money."

"He better be good in bed because if I don't see some money in the next two weeks, you can take care of them at home."

"You gonna fire me? Cause I'd like to see how that works."

She could hear Mary Beth growl and toss something hard against the wall.

"I'll talk to him about it, but I don't think it'll be an issue."

"It better not be. Because I'm starting the paperwork to get us AMI accredited since you're starting your last summer. We're going to need more than twenty-five thousand dollars in excess to get this off the ground."

* * * *

Case's phone rang right as he was leaving to pick up the kids from daycare.

"Case, Ron at Bailey and Howard."

Case hated that in this day and age, with caller ID, people still believed they had to say who they were. Especially since he'd talked to Ron at least a dozen times since his parents passed away, not to mention the fact that Ron was one of the founding partners in Case's father's firm.

"Yes Ron, did you get my packet already?"

"About that," Case's gut clenched so sure he'd have to do more. "We hit a snag."

"What kind of snag?" Case asked. He hated that he had barely two grand left and that might last if he didn't pay utilities, biked to work, and stopped eating.

"Who's Gwen Harris?"

Case raked his brain knowing he'd heard the name before, but couldn't place the face.

"I don't remember."

"She's claiming to be your aunt."

"Mom's sister. I totally forgot about her. She's kind of the pariah of the family."

"She says the twins are hers."

"I saw my mom when she was pregnant."

"Were you there for the conception?"

"No, my parents chose to psychologically damage me in other ways."

"Gwen is claiming your parents used her eggs."

"That's impossible. My parents had given up fertility treatments. If they would have used her eggs it would have been when I was in junior high."

"She's demanding a DNA test and wants to take the kids."

"She's a flake. The reason I didn't recognize the name is because she's never lived in any one place for more than six months. No. They're my kids. I'm their dad now. Aunt Gwen didn't even have the decency to show up at my parents' funeral. Stop this now, Ron."

"You feel that strongly about this? You've been hemming and hawing about taking over guardianship. Frankly, I was surprised you wanted to do a full adoption."

"I'm not breaking up our family. They're young enough and are already saying I'm their dad. I can't give them up to a stranger who doesn't..." Case punched the roof of his car to calm himself down. "Ron, fix this."

"Do you have a girlfriend?"

"A... Why?"

"Because if you were close to being married, creating a stable home—you get the picture."

Case flashed to that morning in bed with Claire and Gabbie both curled up in his arms. Now he was desperate. But he had to do what was right.

"No Ron, I don't have anyone like that right now. But neither does Gwen."

"Gwen Harris was married three months ago to a Wall Street corporate attorney. She's got money, power and she's not afraid of a DNA test to prove she's the twin's biological mother. What are the chances your parents conceived the kids naturally?"

"My mother had two miscarriages before they started going to the infertility doctor. And I know I was natural."

Case had made it to the daycare center. He could feel the tears forming in his eyes. Not only could he lose his kids, he may never see them again. The one person he needed wasn't talking to him. Not because she didn't care, but because she cared too much.

"Ron, I don't care if it's true or not. They're my son and daughter now."

"I just needed to know how to proceed. Do you have anyone that can testify on Gwen's character? Or on your parenting skill? We need to prove you're the best for Claire and Charlie."

"My grandparents are in their seventies, but my grandmother has a bad heart and my grandfather has emphysema. The last thing they need is to be dragged back up here from Arizona to be in the middle of a family quarrel. I'll work on getting someone to testify on my behalf, but it's only been a few weeks."

"Better than Gwen who's at zero, right?"

"You're the expert."

Case hung up and shook the steering wheel violently. All he wanted to do was find a gym and hoop for the next three hours—anything to exhaust himself. But if he wanted the kids, he'd have to put aside his anger. As he walked in, he looked at Gabbie's office, but it was dark. Case suppressed his rage, walked into the toddler room, and was attacked with hugs and kisses.

As he listened to Claire and Charlie tell all about their adventures, he didn't see a reason to rush. Getting their coats and rushing home seemed to be a waste of time. Instead, he sat cross-legged on the floor and let them run around the room bringing him pictures, toys and books as they retold the story of how they spent their day.

When he got the exhausted look from Mandy, he got the point. It was time to go, but that didn't stop the babbling of the kids. Case sopped up every comment like a sponge, saving every moment as if it was his last. That night, the kids helped set the table for dinner and bath time was a breeze.

After the kids were passed out, he sat in the rocker in-between the two toddler beds and watched them sleep for at least an hour before he passed out in the ridged chair too.

Chapter Four

"Happiness is having a large, loving, caring, close-knit family in another city."

—*George Burns*

"Dad, you up for a dinner with your favorite daughter?" Gabbie asked as she kept her back to the front door of the center.

Case would be picking up the twins soon and she'd spent the last week lurking around corners so she could still see him when he picked up Claire and Charlie. She was sure he wasn't catching her. Or at least she hoped so. The dreams she'd been having about him had made her sleep restless so her temper wasn't where she wanted it to be either.

"Tonight?" he asked. "Tonight I was going to be swapping out the windows. It's supposed to be warming up in the next week or so."

"Wow, I can't even get my own father to pick me over windows."

"Now that's not fair. Hey, why don't we order pizza and you can help your old man so I don't break a hip."

"Dad, you're fifty-three and in better shape than me."

"Then you should help me so you can be in as good of shape at fifty-three-years old."

"Alright, pizza?"

"Am I made of money?"

"And Bee teached us hows to writes a C," Claire said in the lobby.

Gabbie's heart caught and she so wanted to be there with the Thomases. Her throat burned. It'd been almost two weeks and Case hadn't even called her cell phone to say hi. He had been desperate, and all Gabbie wanted was for the love she felt to go away. But it couldn't with Claire and Charlie around to remind her of what she had lost.

"You there, Gabbert?" her father asked with his favorite pet name.

"Sorry dad. Just a little kid saying goodbye. Fine, I'll splurge on a large pepperoni."

"Don't forget the breadsticks."

Hanging up, Gabbie knew Case was gone now and she was free to roam the building. But knowledge wasn't going to reduce the pain she had felt since Case dropped her at her apartment building two weeks ago. Case wouldn't even look at her. He seemed so upset that she'd asked him to examine his real feelings for her. Even Charlie and Claire could tell. They were so quiet, like they could feel a tornado brewing and wanted to be lookouts. Gabbie just wished her suspicions about his motivations were wrong.

Driving to her dad's house, Gabbie tried to push past the pain she was feeling. Her dad could always tell when she was upset and would drag it out of her.

"It's about time," her dad said as he pulled the last of the screens out of the tuck-under garage from their nineteen eighties split level home. It was like every other one in their cul-de-sac except theirs was yellow with green shutters.

Gabbie got out and gave her dad a hug. He was a burly guy, an auto mechanic that seemed to always have grease in the cracks of his knuckles no matter how much he scrubbed. A slight potbelly helped balance out his five eight frame topped off with a thick head of silver hair.

He'd raised Gabbie by himself since she was seven and her mother abandoned them both for a guy she'd met at the travel agency she worked for. Gabbie could remember the lost look on her father's face when he had to help her get a dress for a Christmas concert—almost as bad as Case's looking for diapers.

Gabbie brought the pizza in and dropped it on the faux wood counter in the kitchen. Her dad followed up behind her and snagged a slice of pepperoni before she even got the plates out.

"Teenager," she growled at him.

"Whateves yo," her dad mocked.

"How's work?" she asked, knowing the question would distract him from asking about her.

"Got this sixty-nine Impala that Ricky... You remember Ricky, right?" he asked and she nodded.

Like she would ever forget her dad's best friend when he wasn't trying to run some get-rich-quick deal. He'd done them all, Melaleuca, Amway, Cutco, Herbalife, Zango, she'd been secretly hoping he'd sell Avon—the thought of big old Ricky peddling lip gloss and concealer was enough to make her buy some if he demo'ed it.

"He found it at a police auction, got it for a song. A song I tell you. It's a rusted POS, but under the hood it's got a damn three-fifty. You ever hear of such a thing?"

Yes, she had, a dozen times before. Her dad usually was stuck working on newer cars that he hated. Any muscle car got him going. He always had one or two on blocks in the driveway that he'd fix up and sell on the side.

"Look at me yammering on. What about you? What's new? How's school?"

"School's good," she answered and got a drink.

"Somethin' up puddin cup?"

"No."

"Look me in the eye and say that," he said, picking up on her lie.

"No," Gabbie said with her head buried in the fridge.

"Gabs, *you* called me for dinner."

"I just met someone, and it doesn't look like it'll work out."

"That's a shame. Well at least you still got me to be your best guy."

"That makes me the luckiest girl in the world," she said with a smile as they headed out to take off the storm windows and put up the screens.

With two windows swapped out, Gabbie's dad decided it was time to finish the discussion from the kitchen. The thing Gabbie loved about her dad was he didn't push, but he never let her get away with stuff either.

"You want me to tell you how to woo the men?" her dad joked.

"When was the last time you let someone woo you?" she chided back.

"About that..." her dad said breathing in deep and stepping away from the window they were going to take down. "I met someone. I wasn't sure if I should tell you or not."

"Why not?" Gabbie asked and pointed back to the window so they could take down the storm window.

"I don't know. I guess I thought you'd have been upset. I know you always thought your mom would come back."

"When was the last time I even talked about Linda?" Gabbie asked, not about to call the woman who abandoned her mother.

"Now, Gabbie, that's your mother."

"When was the last time you dated anyone?" Gabbie asked as they lowered the storm window to the ground.

"I couldn't date anyone when you were younger."

"Why not?"

"I didn't think you would have understood."

"When I was in elementary sure, but in high school, I wouldn't have cared." Gabbie wiped her forehead with her gloved hand and looked at her dad. "What would you think if I dated a guy with kids?"

"Plural? As in more than one child? Someone that irresponsible…"

"It's not like he has a handful of baby mamas running around."

"This the guy that it's not going to work out with?"

"I'm still holding a small candle burning."

"You're too much like me, but I guess it would depend on the guy."

"So, if he was adopting his twin brother and sister because his parents passed away…"

"The kids in high school?"

"They're two."

"You a cat now, going after young guys?"

"A cougar? No, he's twenty-four."

"Your age? Maybe it's for the best, Gabbert. Think about the kids."

"I am. That's why I told him I couldn't see him."

"He didn't turn you away. I like him already," her dad said as he attached the screen. "So let me get this straight in my old melon. You like him and he likes you."

"Yes."

"Sounds like a disaster waiting to happen. I was hoping you'd go for some jerk that treated you like crap," her dad teased and walked around to the side of the house.

"On me, sarcasm is adorable."

"Now you know why I have women busting down my door. You get your adorableness from me."

Gabbie remembered the desire she'd seen in Case's eyes and a chill ran through her as she once again imagined his touch. Maybe she was deluding herself. It'd been weeks since he'd even spoken to her. How could she have ever foreseen her dad's words were more than simple fatherly advice?

* * * *

Case had seen Gabbie in her office on the phone when he picked up the twins. He imagined a thousand scenarios of who she could be talking to—men being his worst fear. Claire and Charlie had spent the last week talking about her. He wished love was like a chemical formula. The sexy atoms create an ionic bond with intelligence and finally you titrate with caring. The expected output would be the woman of his dreams understanding his love was not a fluke. And that woman would have jet-black hair, gray eyes and be named Gabbie Vaulst.

Every time he rethought the formula in his mind, it came out the same. His scientific theory was flawless. He couldn't imagine anything better than to have Gabbie in his life, but it's not like he could just walk up to her and show her that his experiment hadn't exploded in the lab.

After he had gotten the kids to bed, the home phone rang. He'd forgotten there even was one.

"Hello?"

"Hey, baby, how's my grandbaby doin' today?" his grandmother from his mom's side said.

"Good Nana," he said, happy to hear her voice again. "How have you been?"

"Oh, you know how it is. How's the little ones? Can I talk to them?"

"They're in bed, Nana, it's almost nine here."

"I know. I'm just surprised you got them to bed."

"A lot's changing."

"That's good. Now you keepin' those babies, right? That's your blood."

"Yes, Nana. I'm keeping them."

"That's a good boy," she said in her calm voice.

41

"Nana?"

"Yes, baby?"

"I was thinking of being their father, you know…adopting them."

"What are you gonna tell 'em about your parents?"

"I suppose I'd tell them the truth, but I want them to feel stable and I think calling me dad would help them."

"It don't matter what they call you. It's how you see them. You see them as your babies, they'll feel love. I'm just glad you're takin' care of them. God knows your papa and I couldn't do it."

Case wanted to ask about Gwen. He wanted to know if they knew about his mom using Gwen's eggs, but he couldn't bring himself to add that burden on them.

They spent the next half hour talking about his grandfather's trips to the hospital for treatments, the twins, and his adventures learning to be a dad. Nana had suggestions which he added to his internal rolodex. It took him that long to bring himself to the topic of Gabbie.

"Nana, what do you think about me dating women around the kids?"

"Like I know. I've been with your papa so damn long I don't understand those things. But I would say it'd be nice to be a real great grandmother someday before I die."

"No pressure on me though."

"Of course not. But I won't be around long enough for them babies to give me any. You're my only hope."

He loved his grandmother's guilt trips. They were the best.

"Is there any type of girl you wouldn't want me with?"

"I don't like those girls on the videos—shakin' their butts like they got a rash. But I think my little Case is talkin' about someone or something in particular. If it's someone, I have to wonder if he's like his father. Because I saw that one first hand and you're going to lose your ever lovin' mind."

"Don't let that girl steal your nature, son." His grandfather had picked up the extension at their home.

"Teddy don't you start. Always talkin' mess," his Nana said.

"Get off the phone, girl. This is man talk. We both know the boy's daddy wasn't a player. But my grandson's a player. Daddy was a player, grandpa too, poor boy don't know what else to do."

"You old fool, you just said his daddy wasn't a player. You don't even know what's falling out your lips anymore. Ignore the old fool Case. You like the girl that's all that matters to us."

"She got a big booty?" his papa asked.

"Teddy, don't you start."

"I said, get off the phone, woman."

Case might as well have not been there. It would be at least five minutes before they would notice if he'd hung up. But instead he smiled listening to them picking with each other over what was best for all their grandbabies. His grandfather said that the woman has to have a good booty or Case would get bored. Then it turned to the love Case had had when his parents were alive.

"You know, if you wouldn't have had that booty I'd have never stayed with your nagging butt."

"You two want to let me go? You can fight in the same room and not have to worry about long distance."

"Case, you do what's best for you and those little ones," his nana said, and after a few love yous they hung up.

Case walked to the entertainment center and looked at the picture of his parents together. The way his dad talked about his mom never made sense to him. In high school and college, Case did play the field. He thought his parents didn't know anything about relationships because they had been together forever. Now he knew they were what a relationship was supposed to be.

He'd always tried to control the woman he'd been with so they couldn't make the relationship something he didn't want. Here he was, playing by Gabbie's rules. Was it because she was looking out for his kids? Or because for the first time he was willing to work with someone rather than change them into what he thought he wanted them to be?

Maybe it was because Gabbie was already what he wanted.

Chapter Five

"I wondered if this was how Dorothy felt when she woke up in Oz with all the little people squawking ding dong, the witch is dead."
—Lorraine Beaumont

Case hated dropping off the twins every morning. Not only had Gabbie been a virtual ghost at the facility since they last talked, but he had started to get nasty looks from some of her partners. He was sure it was because of money, not that any of them had the nerve to say anything to him.

Finally, at ten o'clock he got the phone call at work he'd been waiting for.

"This is Case," he said, answering his phone.

"Case, Ron at Bailey and Howard."

"Yeah Ron, are we settled?"

"We're getting there. I got the trust funds released enough to send out bills. However, they have to be filtered through me. Because of the custody issue, you don't have direct access."

"That's fine as long as you can pay for daycare and send me a little money for food, diapers and the utilities."

"Yeah, about that…" Ron's tone made Case's stomach knot up. "I need receipts or invoices to add to the file."

"I don't have receipts from the grocery store."

"But you have bills right?"

Did he have bills? Only a stack as long as his leg.

"Yeah, I got bills. Can you prepay for things? Like daycare and whatnot?"

"Sure, if you're happy with the place and know they'll be there for a

44

while. Up to six months in advance, just like insurance. The house is officially in all your names, so I can pull two-thirds of the property tax out of the trust fund, but you're going to have to come up with the other third."

"How much?"

"About three grand a year. Suburbs, they'll kill you on taxes."

"Three grand. Are you kidding me?"

"How much was rent?"

He had a point there. And he wasn't going to lose his parents' home, especially since it was paid for and in a gated community in Woodbury.

"Fine. When's it due?"

"Not until July first, so you're clear."

"Life insurance?"

"Month maybe…you got enough to get by until then?"

"I'll make it work," Case said. "Where's my aunt at with her claim?"

"I'm waiting on her attorney to set up a DNA test at a place we both agree on. I'm not taking any chances at some cut-rate place. I told them any one of the hospitals in town. They're pushing for a private facility."

"Why?"

"Personally, I think we called her bluff. She's got a new husband, wants to tie him down with a few kids, but doesn't feel like carrying them. Just a theory, I'm not understanding their reactions."

"If you're right, I'll give you a big ole' kiss on the lips."

"You're not my type, but I'll take a hug."

"I knew you were a hugger," Case replied, feeling good for the first time in weeks.

After Ron hung up, Case realized he should have had Ron call the daycare center directly, instead he was going to have to run the risk of Gabbie answering the phone.

"Growing Strong Daycare. This is Gabbie, how can I help you?"

Her voice made Case's heart race. It'd been over two weeks since he'd heard her speak. Her caring voice washed over him with warmth he wasn't prepared for.

"Hello?"

"Um…yeah, Gabbie, it's Case."

He could hear her breathing, but she seemed to lose her light tone.

"How are you?" she asked solemnly.

"Fine, look the trust fund is open, but I'll need you to get my attorney an invoice. I told Ron to pay for six months worth of daycare, but could you do me a favor?"

Again, silence made Case hate he'd been gone from her so long. Maybe it had only been a few seconds, but he could hear the clock ticking behind him until her voice came through the phone again.

"You know I will. How can I help you?"

"I have groceries next week, but I'm almost on empty and the way the fund works I have to send in receipts and prove it was for the twins. Could you tack on a miscellaneous grocery charge to the bill? If you give me the money when the check clears I'll go pick up the groceries."

"That doesn't sound like a bad deal. How about this? I'll put on four and note the account that due to a guardianship clause this is how we need to get the groceries. We do weirder things with some of the other kids."

"Thank you. Um, Gabbie?"

"Yeah?" Her voice was so sweet, and he could envision her with the small strands of hair falling around her face.

Tell her you want her, he urged himself.

"How are the kids today?"

"Charlie drew the cutest picture of you… Have you been able to play basketball with them?"

"Yeah." Case chuckled and knew he wanted to find a way to keep her on the phone longer. He loved the way he felt the weight that had been sitting on his chest lessen with each word.

"Claire and I had lunch together. She invited me to eat with her."

"She did?"

"Yes. It was very sweet. 'Bee lunch peas,' she said while she pulled me across the room."

"They have been doing so well at home. I can't help but think you guys are the reason."

"Don't count yourself out on that. If you weren't reinforcing the lessons, they wouldn't be progressing as much."

Hearing Gabbie's voice was the last push he needed. He was going to make his move. His life was now filled with last chances and hung by a thread. And he wasn't about to cut the thread with Gabbie. If there was anything in his world he was certain about, it was Gabbie Vaulst.

* * * *

Case rushed through the doors of the daycare center as if on a mission. Gabbie was talking to Mandy, and a few of the mothers were picking up their children in the lobby when he took Gabbie's face into his hands and kissed with a passion that shook her to her knees.

As his velvet tongue was delving into her yearning mouth, she lost all thoughts of decorum. All those near misses, all those fantasies she'd been having held no weight against the feel of his lips on hers. His fingers tangled in her hair that she had left down and just when she thought she was going to explode, he separated their lips, but still held her close.

"There will never be a perfect moment to kiss you. I have two kids now that will destroy any romance I try to bring into your life. But I will bring it as often as I can because you're the first thing ever that instantly felt right. And it isn't for the last few weeks. It's for the last few years. If I'd met you a year ago I would have felt the same way I do right now. I want you. I hope you can handle me and all issues I have right now because I'll give up a lot, but I won't give up you."

"Marry him. Marry him now," Mandy ordered and Gabbie slapped her away but kept her eyes locked on Case's.

"Can we go to my office, please?" Gabbie whispered against Case's lips.

For the first time, Gabbie hated having a full glass door on her office. She wanted more and she wanted it now. Case sat on the edge of her desk as she sat in her chair. Flushed and overwhelmed, Gabbie tried to regain some semblance of composure.

Case had just kissed her socks off. Now the dark smell of his cologne filled her small office. She could feel the heat of his body to the left of her as she stared blankly at a learning tools catalog on her desk. Her tongue swept across her upper lip in an attempt to rewet them only to taste the last of Case that was still on her body.

"What took you so long?" she asked when she could speak

coherently again.

"If I'd have carried you into the bathroom or some other kid free zone any sooner than now you wouldn't have believed me.'

"Don't ever make me wait that long again. I say stupid things all the time you know."

There was a knock on her door, and Mandy popped her head in.

"If you guys need a babysitter tonight…"

Gabbie picked up her stress ball off the desk and whipped it at Mandy's head.

"Out," Gabbie snapped

"We could have used that," Case said, frustrated.

"I want a quiet night at home."

"Whose house you going to? Because it's a party every night at my place. We got Elmo DJ'ing the dance floor and all the finest in chicken nuggets."

Gabbie looked down to hide her smile. He meant it. She could tell in his eyes he wanted to be with her, not a surrogate mother.

"I have a lecture to attend tonight at the center. I'll be done around nine. Do you think you'll have them tucked away by then?"

"In bed by eight o'clock," Case said, beaming with pride. "I got this dad thing down."

Gabbie got up by placing her hands on Case's thighs. He sucked in and held his breath as she nestled in between his legs and wrapped her arms around his neck.

"Then by nine-thirty I want dinner waiting for me."

"What do you want?"

"Something that will give you enough energy."

"I'll take a nap while I wait for you."

"You'll wait for me?"

"As long as you need me to, but I'll never keep you waiting again."

Gabbie couldn't believe someone as wonderful as Case wanted her. She leaned in to get one more kiss, and he was more than obliging as his hands traveled down her back and squeezed her ass.

"Please say this will be mine tonight."

"That all you want?"

"Not by a long shot."

"Go get your kids," she said, happily receiving one more light peck from him.

"Will do."

When he walked out of her office, she collapsed back into her chair and spun her back towards the door. After about five minutes her door creaked when it opened and she turned to see Mary Beth's glare.

Gabbie's high was not going to be crushed by anyone.

"We're at almost seven-fifty owed by the Thomases," Mary Beth snapped.

"Actually, if you check the account, they just deposited sixty-eight hundred dollars. Six months worth of daycare paid for and we'll have to draw four checks to them when they have to pick up groceries because a food allowance was prepaid—something with the rules of his guardianship and trust fund."

Mary Beth started getting mad. Her face turned bright red, matching her pixie cut hair. This just didn't make sense. Why would she be upset? When she burst into tears, Gabbie jumped up and closed the office door.

"What is going on?"

"Nate. He's getting married. And his whore is saying he needs to go to college and really shouldn't have to pay any support. Sure I could get by without his money. It's not like I get much anyway. But why should I have to? I wanted to go to college too damn it. I'll be thirty-five before I can."

"You'll be able to go way before then."

"How? I can't go to the training center because who's gonna watch Lukey? I can't have you guys do it because you'll be there too. And Nate's always too busy to deal with Luke outside of a few hours on the weekend. Gabbie, I feel so damn trapped and I don't want to hate Luke. He's my baby."

"You're the business end more than the teaching end. Why don't you go to Century during the day? You do half the office crap at night anyway."

"I can't carry a class load and work. I'm already taking a discount on Luke's daycare bill."

"That is true. We should beat you for keeping us above water and taking such advantage," Gabbie said and Mary Beth nodded in agreement. "Is it crack or meth you're on?"

"What?" Mary Beth said, aghast.

"You keep us going. You know that, right? Why do you always act like you're a burden to us?"

"I didn't put a penny into the start up and Luke's been a free rider for so long. I know you Mandy and Sarah would have taken the student loans and gone to college. I was stupid."

"We've never blamed you. In fact, besides Mandy, we're in a much better place because of you two. Think about it. We'd have gone, gotten drunk, probably flunked out or gotten date raped by a frat guy."

Mary Beth wiped away her tears and sniffled.

"You guys mean everything to me. After my parents kicked me out I was so scared."

"My dad was much happier with spending the little money I had in my college fund on this place than one year of college. It's not like any of us got full rides. Mary Beth, Luke is the best thing that happened to all of us. Stop being the damn victim, fix your hair and let Mandy take Luke for the night. She's offering daycare services." *That'll teach her for bustin' in my office.*

"Really?"

"Take a bubble bath or get slutted up and go to the bar. I don't care, but do something for you. Please."

With bloodshot hazel eyes, Mary Beth turned to Gabbie.

"What's with you and the black Adonis?"

"He is quite statuesque isn't he?" Gabbie said, tilting her head and remembering him shirtless in the bathroom. Her mind went right to the bubbles she flicked at him sliding down his tight abs. She started to warm and imagined what he might have in store for her tonight.

"The things I'd like to do with him," Mary Beth said, getting lost in her own tawdry thoughts. Now Gabbie was pissed, but her stress ball had already been used on Mandy. "Is it bad I miss Nate?"

"It's been that long?" Gabbie asked then was shocked by Mary Beth's response.

"Not as long as it should be. Am I slut for sleeping with a guy who's about to be married?"

"Why are you sleeping with him?"

"I don't know. He's the father of my child. I drop Luke off for his visit and somehow Nate talks me into a quickie. Same thing when I pick Luke up and he 'happens' to be taking a nap."

"He's the cheap ass that convinced you he couldn't feel anything with a condom even though your parents wouldn't allow you to be on the pill. Mary Beth, you need to find someone new. Nate already did," Gabbie stated plainly.

"Oh, God, what am I doing?" Mary Beth said, burying her head in her hands. "That's it. I'm taking Mandy up on her offer. I need to figure out what I'm doing with my life."

Chapter Six

"I'm selfish, impatient and a little insecure. I make mistakes, I am out of control and at times hard to handle. But if you can't handle me at my worst, then you sure as hell don't deserve me at my best."
—Marilyn Monroe

Gabbie left the daycare center and headed to class. During the lecture her mind kept wandering and she knew whatever she'd been taught wasn't registering. When they took a break, she talked to a friend and made up an excuse why she couldn't finish. The fifteen-minute trip to Woodbury seemed too damn long.

It was only eight-twenty when Gabbie knocked on Case's door. She didn't want to ring the bell in case he actually got the kids to sleep. Case opened the door and became really nervous.

"What are you doing here?" he asked as he stepped out onto the porch and pulled the door almost shut behind him.

"I skipped the second half of class. I just thought we'd put this night off long enough. I can come back later..."

"No," he said and looked over his shoulder. "It's just I'm not done cooking yet."

"You're cooking for me?" Gabbie asked, taking a step closer as she wrapped her fingers around the buttons of Case's yellow polo. "I could kiss you for that. I thought I'd be getting pizza."

"A kiss for a meal, not sure if that's an even trade," Case growled.

"It does seem to be lacking a little on my end, huh?"

Case's fingers ran through Gabbie's hair as he lightly brushed his lips against hers.

"How 'bout you run home and get something sexy to wear while I finish dinner?"

"How 'bout we skip dinner and I let you take off my very unsexy teacher clothes?" Gabbie replied.

"No, Baby Girl. I've been working really hard…"

"Case," a woman's voice said as the door behind them opened. "Oh, I'm sorry to interrupt, but where do you keep the honey?"

"I think it's in the back of the spice cabinet," Case said as Gabbie peered around him to look at this girl that was helping him cook.

She could have been a model standing in designer jeans torn in all the right places. A short cami showed her flat stomach with a little diamond stud in her belly button and three smaller diamonds dangling. She looked at Gabbie then tucked her straight, long, honey brown hair behind her ear.

"No," Gabbie said, letting go of Case's shirt and stepping backwards toward her car. "You didn't have to lie to me," she said, pushing Case's chest. "I could have accepted you not wanting me. That I'd understand, but why did you have to lie to me?"

"Gabbie, I thought you weren't going to be here until nine-thirty."

Gabbie's head swirled with thoughts of stupidity. She couldn't believe she fell for this same shit again. How many times had she avoided everyone just to not have to feel the pain she was in at this moment?

"So much for your nap. Or is that what you call sex with a…a…" she scanned the girl who stared blankly at her. "How old are you?"

"Seventeen."

"Seventeen, she's illegal. I hope it was worth it."

Gabbie turned and started to leave when Case wrapped both of his arms around her waist. Trapping her wrists in his hands he held her as she kicked and screamed. Her heart was pounding out of her chest as she saw herself alone forever, unlovable by anyone. She wanted to get away, hit a ball as hard as she could, but Case was tightening around her like a boa constrictor.

"You want to keep making an ass of yourself or would you like to meet my neighbor, Madison?"

"Your neighbor?"

"The twins' babysitter on occasion and daughter of Linc De'Amante."

"That supposed to mean something to me."

"Linc's one of the premier chefs in the city—runs three of the top restaurants in downtown Minneapolis. She was helping me cook you dinner."

Gabbie stopped fighting and Case placed her back on the ground.

"You calm now?"

"No, I'm embarrassed as hell and want to run away."

"Not going to happen."

"I ruined our evening by acting like a dumb child."

Case turned around still holding on to Gabbie's waist and she looked at the very confused girl in front of her.

"Madison, this is my girl, Gabbie."

Gabbie now felt even smaller. He introduced her as his actual girlfriend. Not his friend. Not the twin's babysitter, but his girl.

"Nice to meet you," she said extending her hand. Case released his right arm so Gabbie could shake. "Case has been talking non-stop about you for the past few weeks."

And now Gabbie was wishing for the power to turn into a pile of dust and blow away.

"I'd say it was nice to meet you, but right now I want to put my head in an oven."

"Don't worry about it. If I'd walked in on the same thing with my boyfriend...I'm sure I might have spazzed out too."

Great, Gabbie thought. *I've gone from the weird cat lady to a teenager in the span of a day.*

"Case, I can finish the glaze if you two want to talk."

"I think that'd be great."

When Madison had gone back in the house, Case sat Gabbie down on the porch swing. For a few minutes they just rocked. Gabbie knew she'd have to speak first, she just didn't know how to justify her behavior.

"You get jealous easy?" Case asked while they both stayed focused on the brick wall in front of them next to the front door.

"Not normally. Although I've thought of killing one of my partners today after she made a comment, so I'm going to blame it on you and lack of sex."

"That's probably for the best. No fault on you at all."

"No, I'm blameless in the world—perfect in every way."

"I might start thinking you like me, seeing as you're going postal on any woman that breathes in my general direction."

"I've never freaked out like that before."

"I've seen worse, but can you never do that again?"

"Can't promise."

"I broke up with my last girlfriend for a lot of reasons, but the biggest was she would snap on any girl that came near me. I found out it was because she was cheating so I must be too…at least in her mind."

"Technically I snapped on you, not Madison."

Case and Gabbie both turned and looked at each other.

"I guess that would be an improvement from Sasha."

"You could have told me," Gabbie suggested.

"That I had someone over to help me cook your surprise dinner. How does that work again?"

"You know, pointing out flaws in my insanity doesn't make up for upsetting me."

"You're really making me the bad guy in this?" Case said with a chuckle.

"It helps me cope with the fact that I'm a dumb ass and you'll probably never want to see me again."

"I do like the jealousy," Case said holding up his index finger and thumb about an inch apart. "A little bit, but Gabbie…"

"I know. I have no claim to you."

"Is that both ways? Because I thought you did and I did."

"You meant it. I'm your girl?" Gabbie asked as a knot started to form in her gut. Sure she'd obsessed about Case since the second they met, but do people really lay claim to each other that fast?

"The most frustrating girl I know. And I have a two-year-old that should be renamed Princess Diva living in my house. So Queen Diva the First, I see now I have to be very clear with you from now on. I want you to be my girl. I want to be your man."

"Why am I a girl and you're a man?"

"I want you to be my woman," Case clarified and Gabbie crawled onto his lap.

"If I'm your woman..." she said while pulling out the binder that held back his dreads.

"Yes," he replied his naturally deep bass voice growled.

"Then I need you to treat me like your woman, tonight, so I forgive you for making me act like a dumb ass."

"They don't teach you logic at the school you go to, do they?"

"Have you tried to reason with a four-year-old on a regular basis?"

Gabbie caught his full lips with hers and then nipped at his bottom lip with her teeth. As his arms encircled her body, she hoped he could bring her the pleasure she'd heard existed in the world. But if not, being held by him was enough to make her feel safe.

Chapter Seven

"Some people are settling down, some people are settling and some people refuse to settle for anything less than butterflies."
—Carrie Bradshaw; Sex in the City

"This is kinda our first date," Case said and Gabbie caught a chill.

She cut a piece of chicken off and kept her eyes down. Looking at the plate, she could tell Madison's dad was master chef. On the plate was a large lettuce leaf with a cross-hatched grilled chicken breast. There was a raspberry marinade drizzled over the plate and three bright red raspberries sitting on the edge. On the opposite side of the plate were long green beans with a honey and raspberry glaze on them. A small dollop of risotto made up the third point in the triangle that surrounded the chicken breast. Sweet and succulent would be an accurate description of the meat.

"Gabbie?"

"It's sad, I slept with you before our first date."

She kept her eyes down. For some reason, the idea of a formal date seemed like a tremendous amount of pressure. Why couldn't he have just done his business with her in the bedroom and then they could move into an awkward relationship that included two adorable children?

Because that's not a relationship, she reminded herself. But that's what she understood.

Case laughed at her comment, but she still wasn't at ease. Sure at *McDonalds* she could stuff her face with a sandwich and fries then chase kids through a tube, but talking. Conversing. Adult conversation. How the hell could she do that?

"Gabbie are you okay?"

"I'm sorry," she said, finally swallowing and looking at him. "I've never really dated…I don't understand the first date thing. The last guy I went on a date with was Homecoming, senior year."

Case set down his utensils and looked at her. His head tilted to the side as if he was trying to processes some strange information.

"Why?"

"Why what?"

"Why haven't you dated anyone?"

"I've been busy."

"No one's that busy."

"I was. Anyway guys don't…" She paused and moved the food around the plate.

"Don't what?"

"Talk to me, usually."

"Do you talk to guys?"

"Not usually. You had a buffer," she explained

"Charlie?"

"Yeah. He bridged my fear."

Case cut another piece off his chicken and smiled. Holding his fork to his lips, he shook his head and said, "I knew kids were a chick magnet."

"I wasn't drawn to you by some adorable baby juju."

"You weren't?" he asked leaning on his forearms.

Gabbie saw his biceps flex and her breath caught. What was it about Case that could set her at ease one second then send her stomach into a tailspin a minute later? She didn't belong with him. He belonged with some Halle Berry or Heidi Klum type. Tall, lean with perfect skin and a smile that could light up any party. He needed a woman on his arm that would complement him, not make people gawk in confusion. This was a mistake. Her jealousy over anyone touching him was pushing her over the edge one minute, then she was fumbling over herself the next, trying to not feel insecure.

How many days could she keep up with him? She didn't know what she was doing in the bedroom that could possibly satisfy a man. Sure, she'd read romance novels. She'd seen all the movie love scenes, but that was fiction. Gabbie had learned first hand more than once that sensual romance didn't exist.

Are we doing this or not? Kirk had snapped at her on a date. Why she let herself be used by him, she'd never understand. He was cute too. Long blond hair always fell in his eyes and she loved clearing it even though he'd snap on her. All the girls wanted him and for the first time she felt she, not Mandy or Mary Beth, was the pretty one. She was the one they were all jealous of and she was the one lying to her best friends about how he would talk to her—playing up the relationship as if it was more than it was.

But she had learned her lesson. She had become a stronger person because of it. She looked across the table at Case and saw something she'd wanted to see for years—desire—the way he stared at her and seemed to drink in her curves. Gabbie liked the way he would eye her neck and then lick his lips. She liked that he got hard when they almost kissed at work. And most of all, she loved that he promised to bring her romance.

What was she so afraid of? He liked her. Gabbie was determined to accept his words, because she deserved to be loved.

"Are you going to tell me or should I guess?" Case asked.

"Huh?" Gabbie replied coming out of her head.

"What drew you to me?" he growled and Gabbie squirmed in her seat.

"I'm not comfortable talking about that."

"Okay how about your last date, what did you do?"

"Went to a dance."

"That it?"

"He didn't make me dinner," she smiled and started to settle into their meal.

"So I got one up on him?"

Gabbie's breath hitched as she drank in Case's smooth dark skin and deep mahogany eyes. She smiled as she looked at his full lips surrounded by the tightly trimmed goatee.

"More than one," she said with a smile.

"After the date, did you see him again?"

"He was my boyfriend for most of senior year."

"And he only took you on one date?"

"It was high school," *and he didn't want to be seen in public with me.* Gabbie recalled.

"What do you consider a date?"

"Time spent together doing an activity."

"You never did anything with him?"

"It was a very one sided relationship. Can we talk about something else?"

"He hurt you, didn't he?"

"Not physically," Gabbie said, spooning the risotto in her mouth so she could say, "at first" without Case hearing it.

"I'm sorry you had a bad boyfriend. But I'm not sorry he made it so you didn't like talking to guys."

Gabbie tried to process what he said but couldn't understand his connotation.

"Why?"

"Because then we wouldn't be here together. I'm sure that any other guy would have fallen as far as I have."

"You've fallen for me?"

"Do you ever hear a thing I say?"

"Yes, but it's nice to hear it repeated."

Case encircled her hand with his. Stroking his thumb across the back of her hand, Gabbie felt the warmth coursing from his hand to hers.

"How often?"

"Often?"

"How many times a day do you want to hear how much you mean to me?"

Gabbie felt the flush cross her cheeks as she looked down at her plate. Case squeezed her hand and she turned her eyes back to his.

"Whenever you think of it. I'd never ask you to force it. I want sincerity most of all."

* * * *

After dinner, Case brought Gabbie to his room. It hadn't changed much since high school. He still had trophies from basketball all the way

60

back to third grade running along the edge of his floor. Since he knew Gabbie was coming over, his bed was actually made with the same navy blue comforter he'd had forever. His clothes were stuffed on the floor of his closed closet and on the walls were a few posters of different NBA players. Looking at them with Gabbie in his room made him think he might need to grow up.

"It would be too weird to sleep in my parents' room right now," he explained. "Maybe someday I'll be able to clean out their stuff."

"These your friends?" Gabbie asked as she looked at a corkboard above his desk with pictures of some of his teammates from his AAU traveling team.

"Yeah, that's Swift, Popeye and Marco."

"Did you have a nickname?"

"Some kids called me Tommy Boy, but not really."

"Oh," she said and crossed her arms in front of her chest.

He could tell she was getting nervous by the way she was nibbling on her bottom lip. During dinner she had calmed down a little bit, but it was obvious she was still ashamed of the way she had acted with Madison. Case was surprised his first reaction was to pull her close instead of letting her storm off. That had been the way he'd always been with Sasha and the parade of other girls in the past. *Act like a child? Find another man to be your daddy.* He didn't have time for childish outbursts in his life. But the thought he'd lose Gabbie stopped him cold. He wanted to have her in his arms.

Case put his iPod on shuffle, hoping to find a song that would calm her down. The first song was *5 Senses* by Jeremiah and he couldn't help but feel it was fate. He walked to Gabbie and used two fingers to take out her hair binder. Her hair cascaded down her back right as the lyrics sang about how beautiful the girl was and how she must taste. Gabbie's eyes became hooded. His fingers trailed down the column of her neck and she trembled.

He took his time undoing each button of her shirt. With each popped clasp he teased her with his lips on her neck—not kissing, just keeping them away from her raised skin, letting his breath tickle her soft flesh. He had to make up to her and seduction was his favorite band-aid. With her shirt open, he moved behind her and let the soft fabric glide down her arms. Her head tilted to the side and he knew he was forgiven for any transgressions she'd made up in her insane mind.

Case moved Gabbie's silken black hair around so it fell forward over her left shoulder and then he kissed her neck right between her shoulders. His fingers tingled as they slid down her back and unhooked her bra. Her head turned and her eyes caught his as she held an arm to her chest because the straps of her bra clung loosely to her arms.

Case took off his shirt and wrapped his arms around her stomach. Gabbie's body was warm against his even though she trembled with each kiss he placed on her bare shoulder.

"Do you know how amazing your body is?" he asked.

She trembled from his touch, but didn't respond.

"Those not-sexy teacher clothes are hiding something that is better than I imagined."

He ran his hand down her arm, surrounded her hand with his and guided her to the bed. Lying on their sides facing each other, Case kissed her. He kept his thumb stroking her jaw as his hand cradled her head. She used the time to feel his abs and slid her hand towards his jeans. His hand caught hers and brought it back up to his chest.

"No," he said against her lips. "This is for you."

Laying her back on the bed, Case let his tongue taste her sweet skin down to her perked nipple. As his mouth surrounded her swollen breast, she moaned and her legs squirmed. His left hand found her knee and hitched her leg to his hip. When secure, his hand glided up the back of her thigh. Her fingers tangled in his loosened dreads.

Case continued to suckle her hardened nipple and Gabbie groaned his name. Cupping her ass, her body fell towards him, but he pushed back so he was on top of her and she was planted firmly on her back. It took him three long caresses to reach the top of her pants. He looked at her with a devilish smile and she responded by holding her breath.

He had to stand up to remove her pants. Well, he didn't have to, but he wanted to see her laid out on his bed in just a pair of light blue cotton panties. They were hi-cut and, on most women, plain. But on Gabbie, the way they cut a path on either side of her legs made it so he couldn't help but crawl over her and kiss her waiting lips. He loved the feel of her hands as they touched his face, keeping the connection between the two of them.

"I want to taste you," he whispered against her lips and she trembled beneath him. "You know this is the first time you've been speechless since we met."

"I'm the student in this."

Case sat back and looked at her. She couldn't mean, no, he couldn't believe what she had just said.

"You're a virgin?"

"No," she said with all the authority of a ten-year-old teaching Organic Chem.

"That wasn't convincing."

"I've had sex. Bad. Quick. I was little more than a receptacle. None of this," she said with her hands moving between their bodies. "I didn't know men really did this."

Case leaned over her again and with a low tone he said, "Real men do. Before we go any further, I need to ask you something personal."

"Okay," she replied shaking against Case's fingertips that were teasing the soft skin of her belly.

"I'm clean, I swear. I got tested after my last girlfriend."

"I'm on birth control, 'cuz…well I don't want to tell you, but…I swear."

"So can I?" Case asked, not wanting to be rude and ask if he could raw dawg it.

"You keep this up, I won't know how to say no to you."

His fingers slid beneath the cotton of her panties as he whispered in her ear.

"Does that include don't stop? Because my goal is to hear that from your trembling lips."

Gabbie didn't think her lips could do anything but tremble around Case after tonight. Never had a man made sure she was pleased at all, let alone first. Case's long fingers started to tickle the soft folds between her thighs and she held her breath again. When his finger slid inside, she couldn't believe he was making her have a reaction.

"No one has ever touched you this way?" Case asked as he kissed her neck.

"I have…" Gabbie gasped for air. "He just never…Oh my God," she moaned in response to him flicking her now swollen nub.

She was trying to fight her embarrassment. All the times Kirk growled at her, *that's disgusting, Gabbie. Girls don't do that.* She was wet as hell and tried to find a way to stop herself. *I thought you were a good girl. Not a slut like your friend, Mandy. I don't know if I even want to touch you.* She had run to the bathroom to try to dry herself off, but that was with Kirk. Now with Case she could only cover her face with her arms.

"They never what?" he asked. His deep voice seemed to vibrate through her chest as he laid on top of her. "Say it, Gabbie. I want to know what I'm doing to you."

Gabbie's breath quickened, but she couldn't say. How could she tell him what he was doing to her? That was too intimate. Too personal. Too… Case increased his pace and placed two more fingers inside her. Gabbie's hips arched against his hand as his fingers stroked inside her sex.

"I know I'm doing something… You're so wet, baby."

"I'm sorry," Gabbie blurted.

"Sorry? For what? Being amazing? I can feel you beginning to come against my fingers."

"I'm not supposed to."

Case's fingers stopped moving but stayed buried inside her. He pulled back and looked at her.

"What aren't you supposed to do?"

"Be like this."

"Why not?"

"Because girls…" Gabbie bit her hand to shut up.

"Girls don't what?"

"It's gross, I know."

"Gross? It's sweet as hell," Case said, staring at her. "I can't wait to taste you. I don't know who you fucked…and I say fucked because any man…strike that—boy that made you this up-tight with a body as fine as yours…didn't know what he was doing."

With his free hand, he stroked her hair back from her eyes and made sure her hands couldn't hide them.

"You're beautiful and let me tell you something. What your body is

64

doing right now is wonderful and turning me on. So please, Gabbie…"
Case stroked against her sex. "Tell me…tell me what I'm doing to you. I
want to know."

Why? She thought. Why would he possibly need to know he had her
experiencing the most sensual feelings she'd ever known? Gabbie looked
in his eyes and was caught when she saw eyes that cared for her. Case
wasn't lost in himself. His pleasure. He wasn't rushing to stick himself
inside her and get it over with. He didn't lie to her, saying girls aren't
supposed to like it. Case was drinking in her reaction. He was deriving
his satisfaction from hers.

"My breasts…" she started. Her eyes closed. Gabbie's voice was
barely audible; she still feared he'd condemn her for being wet or the
shivers that were shooting through her body.

"Yes," he hissed, his fingers delving deeper inside. With each
satisfying stroke she felt herself start to let go.

"They're on fire. And my lips…"

"You mean these soft lips?" he asked placing a soft peck that had
her searching for more only to find he'd pulled away.

"They want you…"

"What do they want from me?"

"They just want to be touching you."

"And what about here?" he asked, his fingers circled inside her.

"Oh Case, I need…" Gabbie groaned as her sex clamped on to his
fingers.

He caressed her lips with tenderness at first, but as his tongue licked
at her lips she opened and stroked his tongue with hers. Running her
fingers through his dreads she couldn't believe how sensual he was with
her. Case's fingers stroked against her core, and she couldn't help but
shiver.

Case left her lips. She wanted to protest, but he was taking care of
her in a way she couldn't understand. His strong lips were creating a trail
down the center of her body with a soft lick every few inches. Her skin
rose goose bumps all over her body and she knew she was falling in
love. When he began to suck and lap at her sex, she pulled back her legs
only to have him lock her thighs onto his shoulders with his strong arms.

With every loving stroke of his tongue, she thought she'd scream.

When he began sucking on her, she snatched the pillow from under her head and moaned into it. As least she hoped it was only a moan. It could have been a scream or yell. Either way it was something that had been buried deep inside her, and when it came out, she felt herself clench. *This is what it must feel like*...Her mind went blank.

Case kissed her hip, then her rib and finally took her aching breast into his mouth. With his other hand, he pushed aside her legs that had snapped shut when his lips left her and she felt his body slide between her thighs.

"You came, didn't you, Baby Girl?" he whispered against her throat.

Gabbie mumbled something she thought was an acknowledgement of his achievement.

"We're just getting started," he warned as he eased his hardened shaft deep inside her.

Gabbie's body arched up into his, and his hands wrapped around her back. Her legs locked around his hips as her fingers curled into fists around the sheet below. After a few grinding strokes, she thought she'd cry from pleasure. His hands went up her back until they were between her shoulders. The heat from his smooth skin wasn't enough to quell the gooseflesh that had erupted across her body.

"I love your body," he said as he rolled her in his bed. "I want to see all of it."

His hips shifted and she surrounded the whole of him. When she was underneath him, she thought she had been filled to capacity. Now she was sure she'd burst and she didn't give a good goddamn.

Gabbie panted, looked down at his dark eyes filled with desire and couldn't believe he was in her life. His hands wandered along her belly, then curled around her hips.

The rhythm of Case's strokes inside Gabbie made her toss her head back. She bit her lips to hold in the scream she had buried deep. Her body trembled and her core clenched him. He was less timid when it came to his release. Case's mouth opened and a roar bounced off the wall as he pulsed inside her. It was as if their sexes were fighting for control of the small space. Looking down at Case she didn't know what to think. They both panted and the connection they'd created was beyond a simple joining of bodies. His eyes were now hooded with satisfaction while his dark lips curled up in a small smile, but behind the droopy eyes Gabbie saw more. So much more than she could have ever imagined.

He pulled her down, curled in behind her and brought the blanket over the two of them.

"Am I forgiven?" he asked as he kissed her shoulder.

"I was mad at you," she replied, having forgotten what had transpired before. "No…No you're not forgiven."

"What? Seriously girl? You gonna stay mad at me?"

"I need that like three, four hundred more times."

"It's not going to happen tonight. I'll top out at ten," he teased back and tickled her ribs.

"Guess you're stuck with me then, cause I know you'd hate to be on my bad side."

"Best punishment I've ever gotten," Case said, hugging Gabbie's body close to his. He let his hand wander down her hip and around to her full ass. "This is not your bad side," he said with a squeeze. "This is your amazing," he kissed the edge of her shoulder. "Sexy," he kissed her collarbone. "Fantastic side," he murmured and kissed the base of her neck.

"You weren't kidding about ten times were you?" she asked, his hardness having returned with a vengeance.

"Fastest recovery time ever. Wonder why?" he asked as his lips found hers and he crawled on top. As Gabbie's legs spread and his hips fell against hers, she drifted into a sedated peace where she no longer questioned his motives. Beyond the physical she felt desired for the first time in her life.

Chapter Eight

*"When you are courting a nice girl an hour seems like a second.
When you sit on a red-hot cinder a second seems like an hour.
That's relativity."*

—*Albert Einstein*

An empty bed was not something Case wanted to wake up to. He had hoped Gabbie would have spent the night, but he understood her stance on the kids. Adult relationships were confusing to kids. You have your mom and dad. That's your anchor. Beyond that—aunts and uncles, family friends, grandparents, but your two main caretakers are who you look to for guidance. And instability of any kind could be unsettling, especially when the kids knew who their parents were.

Now he needed to get up and make breakfast. Somehow he was going to have to do it without thinking about Gabbie's soft, supple hips or her amazingly tight... Whoever slept with her before was a moron. The things that woman could do when inspired.

They had had sex two more times before he passed out. He'd thought they both did, but now he knew better. The only reason he hadn't moved was because he could still smell her plumeria lotion on the pillow next to him. Then he heard a toilet flush and he knew he was outnumbered.

Dragging himself down the hall, he poked his head into the twin's room and found it empty. He could feel the goofy ass grin on his face from a night of satisfaction and tried to hide it. It's not like the kids would know or even understand what had happened, but a part of him couldn't help the need to suppress his outright glee.

Of course, seeing Gabbie in the kitchen feeding the twins at the kitchen island made him lose all control over his lips and the smile on his face was happily matching Gabbie's.

"Oooohh, Ace," Claire said in her normal silly way. "Bee made meal…"

"Oatmeal," Gabbie corrected.

"Omeal," Claire said, then held up a fourth of a piece of toast that was cut long ways. "Wif choo choo twain toast."

"Choo choo train toast," Case said with similar excitement as he nestled in behind Gabbie and placed his hands on her stomach. "I'm surprised you're still here."

"I need to work on my ninja skills. They caught me," Gabbie replied under her breath.

"I'm glad they caught you. I love choo choo train toast," he said softly in Gabbie's ear and felt her skin rise on her neck. "And I love you."

Gabbie's body stiffened. Maybe it was too soon to say it, but he didn't care. He wasn't holding anything back that might take the chance of losing her for another two weeks. The breakfast scene he'd walked in on is one he wanted to see for the rest of his life. Maybe with a few kids of their own mixed in. With Gabbie by his side, he knew anything was possible.

"Case…" she started to say as she braced her hands on the island in front of her.

"You don't have to return it. I needed to say what I felt so there was no confusion between us."

Gabbie turned around in his arms so they could face each other. With her head turned up towards him she uttered the words that made this the best day of his life.

"I love you too."

Which he rewarded with a small kiss as the peanut gallery giggled behind them. The last thing he needed was Charlie to say anything about a mom and dad and have Claire flip out.

"You righ, Arlie, Bee good mama," Claire said, dunking her toast in her oatmeal.

Gabbie's cool gray eyes stared into Case's as she stroked his jaw and pulled his chin closer. Her soft lips touched his and she became the aggressor with her tongue lightly touching his lips which he spread and she explored his mouth, stroking his tongue with hers and bringing them so close that if they wouldn't have been clothed they would have fused together permanently.

"Something tells me you want that?" he asked with all seriousness in his voice.

"I...I don't know if..."

"Is that where you want us to go?"

"Yes," Gabbie replied breathless.

"Good, because that's what I've been thinking about when it comes to you."

"Seriously."

"Not settling for, but settling down."

Gabbie swallowed hard and shook her head. "A few weeks ago I thought I was going to be getting another cat and turning into a spinster teacher."

"That's not what I was thinking about a few weeks ago," Case said, stroking back her hair and tucking it behind her ear. Her head turned into his palm and he leaned into her other ear. "It's about time you caught up. I'm not saying you're a moron, but you do seem a little slow."

Gabbie smacked his arm and they finally broke from their embrace. Case pulled up a stool and sat next to the kids eating his own oatmeal with choo choo train toast that circled his plate.

* * * *

Gabbie stopped at home for a quick shower and to feed a crying Lucy.

"You know Lucy, you never want me here so I don't know why you're complaining now," Gabbie said as she started to leave.

Lucy's bowl was full and she even gave her a five-minute belly rub, which was about four minutes longer than Lucy usually allowed. It was like somehow this cat knew she was being replaced.

At work, Gabbie tried to stay focused even though her body still hummed from her night with Case. She was tempted to look in a thesaurus just to see how many other words she could use to describe him besides amazing. When she took her lunch in her office, an unexpected, but then again very expected, visitor showed up.

"Somebody got some," Mandy sung as she plopped into the chair across the desk from Gabbie, snatching Gabbie's stress ball as she did.

"Are you twelve?" Gabbie asked as she pierced a cucumber in her salad.

"And three quarters," she teased. "Did he do it? Did he find your sweet spot?" Gabbie could feel her face flush. "He did. So is it true what they say about black guys?"

"Like I would have a basis of comparison."

"Compared to Kirk?"

"Kirk made me wonder why we used bananas in health class," Gabbie said, covering her lips with her hand since she still had a mouthful of salad.

"Did Case make it clear to you? Or did he confuse you as to why they didn't go to the state fair and use a prize winning—"

Gabbie cut her off. "You're horrible."

"He did. Come on. I need a little vicarious living."

"Since when? I never asked for any second hand porn from you."

"He was like a porn star? Oh, please tell me more."

"When have I ever shared any sexual exploits with you?"

"You told about Kirk," she reminded Gabbie.

"Actually, I asked if it counted as sex and you made me describe it. Then I remember a lot of laughing. You're lucky I didn't become one of your bicuriosities, the way you scarred me."

"I would have found your sweet spot a lot sooner than age twenty-three."

Gabbie reached for her stress ball, then remembered Mandy was holding it.

"You know you're playing up to a stereotype that drove us crazy in high school."

"Some softball team started the stereotype. I can't help I don't discriminate who I spend time with. It's not like I'm Sarah who hates men all together. And then there's Mary Beth and you, strictly dickly. Is it because you were so good with the bat that you love the feeling of *hardwood* in your hands? By the way, was it?"

"Was what?"

"Case? As big as a bat?"

"You know I hit over five hundred by senior year so you might consider not pissing me off."

"Speaking of hitting…"

"I'm his girl. This isn't a hit it and quit it. So, can we treat my relationship with some respect?"

"Fine. I hate that everyone's growing up without me," Mandy whined.

That's why Gabbie loved her. She was under no delusion of what or who she was. And she still respected her friends' wishes.

When Case picked up the kids Gabbie was there with a kiss and he invited her over again, this time as a family. She explained her cat was losing her mind.

"I want you there in the morning when I wake up. If that means the kids get a pet, we'll make room. Our kids have to all play together sometime," he teased, picking up the picture Gabbie had on her desk of Lucy asleep on her bed. "No time like the present."

There it was. Gabbie's family had been formed.

* * * *

It'd been a week since Gabbie had more or less moved in with Case. The kids loved her cat, even though Lucy spent more time under the bed than anywhere else.

Gabbie had put Charlie and Claire to bed a few minutes before when she walked out to the driveway where Case had started his ritual. When Gabbie didn't have class, he got to shoot hoops. It reinvigorated him.

Shooting from the right wing he hit the rim, but the ball shot to the edge of the garage where Gabbie caught it.

"Wanna play horse?" she asked, then bounced the ball back to Case.

"I prefer one on one," he replied, hitting a jumper from what would be the top of the key. "Unless you're chicken."

Gabbie went under the basket and picked up the ball.

"Check," she said, bouncing the ball to Case.

"I'm not going to take it easy on you."

"Neither will I," she replied, raising her eyebrow and crouching down to a defensive stance.

Case hip-checked Gabbie as he went around her, and hit an easy lay-up. He caught the ball as it dropped through the net and checked it back to Gabbie.

"One nothin'," he said with a smile.

Gabbie dribbled the ball, but stayed in place at the top of the key. Case kept his eyes locked on hers. He tried to read what she was going to do. Sure he could take her off the dribble. She faked right and then dribbled behind her back, drove left to the hole and scored her own left-handed lay-up.

"I thought you played softball," Case said with a smile, having been duped for the first time in years.

"I said I got a scholarship for softball," Gabbie said, shooting a chest pass to Case. "I got too many techs in basketball so I was told I couldn't be on the team if I didn't get myself under control."

Damn if that wasn't the sexiest statement he'd heard in a long time. *How am I supposed to play with a hard on?* At least he still had his height advantage. Refocused on the task at hand, he slowly dribbled out and decided he needed to size up his competition a little better if he was going to win. And he was going to win.

He lobbed the ball to the basket, then got his own allieoop and slam-dunked the basketball. Gabbie crossed her arms as she looked at him hanging on the rim until he jumped down.

The ball had rolled into the lawn. He lightly picked it up and tossed it to her.

"Check."

"It's on like *Donkey Kong* now," she challenged and Case went into his defensive stance.

They went back and forth. He got some steals, but so did she. He decided it must be because she was so short she could take his dribble. Either way, by the time they were tied at twenty-one, both were covered in sweat and panting. The only light was from the outdoor light by the garage and Case had the ball at the top of the key. He held it with his right hand over Gabbie's head. He'd learned the hard way that she'd steal it if he didn't keep it out of her reach.

Gabbie stood with her hands on her hips, catching her breath as well. Her eyes focused on the ball above his head. She sucked in her top lip, then sighed.

"We playin' or you gonna keep auditioning to be the next Statue of Liberty?"

"Time," he said, setting the ball down and taking off his shirt. Then he adjusted his shorts by pulling them up so they fell right at his hips.

Comfortable and no longer feeling encumbered, he knew he could take her to the hole two more times. Right as he was about to time in, Gabbie held up her hand. "You trying to distract me?"

"This?" he questioned as he flexed his abs and let his hand sweep over them. "This distracts you?"

Gabbie licked her top lip and held her breath. *Oh yeah,* Case thought, *I gotcha now, baby.* But Gabbie was not going to be swayed. Her fingers curled around the hem of her light yellow T-shirt as she slowly pulled it over her head.

"You better make it fast before they call the cops," she said, looking down at her chest with the pink lace bra.

Case caught himself licking his lips looking at the bare skin of her stomach misted with sweat and the sweet mounds of flesh being held back by delicate lace. *Shit.*

"That's how it's gonna be?" he asked as he tried to refocus on the orange circle ten feet up. "Fine, time in."

Right as he said "time in" Gabbie rushed him. Her lips locked on his and he wrapped his left arm around her back, but kept the ball above his head with his right arm.

"Good try," he said, dropping her and taking a shot from the corner.

It banked left and Gabbie ran to get the rebound. She stepped outside the designated three-point line and shot.

"You touched my body." Case rushed her after her shot swished through the net. "I call foul."

"No blood, no foul," she giggled, grabbing her shirt and running into the house.

Case caught her in the kitchen, wrapping his arms around her waist and lifting her into his arms. She stroked his cheek and kissed him again.

"We need a shower," she said as his sweat dripped on her nose.

"My parents' shower can hold two people, unless we're too old."

"Lead the way," she said as he brought her into the master bathroom.

Gabbie started the shower and Case ran to his bathroom to get their soaps. When he came into the room, the glass of the oversized shower was already fogged over, but he could make out the dark silhouette of Gabbie. Case dropped his shorts and stepped into the hot water. Gabbie's fingers ran through her now wet hair.

His arms wrapped around her stomach as he stepped in behind her. Her slick body spun in his arms as she came face to face with him. His lips fused with hers and his tongue danced in her mouth. He loved competition and she had stoked a flame inside him.

Pressing her back against the muted Italian tile in the shower, Case rested his forearm against the wall to brace himself. When their lips released, she slid down his body, licking the warm water sprinkled on his dark skin. On her knees in front of him his hardness came right to her lips as they encircled it.

The soft warmth of her mouth made him moan her name as he raised his other arm to fully brace himself. She began stroking the remainder of the shaft that couldn't fit inside her mouth with her right hand. Gabbie's left hand traveled around his hips and her nails drug along his ass, not to be painful, but to tickle and tease.

His eyes fogged over as he tried to focus on Gabbie's luscious pink lips surrounding his dark shaft. With every sucking stroke, he felt himself reaching climax, but held back. Gabbie let go of his hardness and reached for his hips to balance herself as she licked the thick vein under his cock until she came to the tip. Swirling her tongue on the edge, her hand returned as her mouth engulfed him and his gut locked as he came.

Looking down, he was sure she was going to cough or gag or in some way punch him. Instead, she drank what he gave and he dropped his hands into her wet, dark mane, knotting his fingers in the tangles until she fell back gasping for air.

Resting against wet tile, Gabbie covered her face with her hands.

"I don't know what came over me," she mumbled and Case got it. She was embarrassed as hell.

Case collapsed to the floor next to her and pulled her into his arms.

"You okay?" he asked as she kept her head nestled against his chest. She still hadn't looked up at him. "What's the matter, Baby Girl?"

"Nothing." She sighed. "I still need to wash my hair," she said keeping her face nuzzled against his chest.

"Tell me about it," he said, kissing the top of her head.

They sat under the spray for a few minutes when Case made the fatal mistake of letting his fingers stroke Gabbie's arm. Then they fell to her ribs and finally her hip.

"Why is it?" he asked while pulling her body up so she was back on her knees. "That every time I'm with you, I never feel close enough."

"How close we talking?" she asked.

He reached for her leg and brought it to his far side so she was straddling his hips. She didn't slide down over him. Not yet. She'd gotten good at teasing his dumb-ass that seemed to lose control whenever she was around, especially his areas south of the border.

Case licked his bottom lip then caught it with his teeth.

"I need you, all the time," he stated plainly.

"Let's just take advantage of the time we do get," she suggested, then stood up and turned off the water.

"No," Case grumbled as he reached for her hips.

"I didn't say I wasn't going to use this time," she said, turning around and slowly dropping her full booty right in front of his face.

He bit at Gabbie's creamy, white ass cheek and she giggled. Working her way down his body, she slid herself over the stiffened head of his dick while her knees laid flat on either side of his legs. She moaned as she rocked his sex deep inside her. Case surrounded her full breasts in his hands. She was leaning over so he licked his way up her from between her shoulder blades, and when he got to her neck, he pulled both of their bodies up and she didn't miss a beat with her hips.

Fully bounded by her sex, he couldn't help but feel as if he'd hit the lottery. Her moans were an angel's song bouncing around the tiled shower. The way Case sounded coming from her lips as she rode him was enough to make him come. Her core shivered, then clung to him and every inch of her flushed pink.

"Gabbie," he growled.

He could feel his sack tightening and every nerve seemed to explode at once as he pulsed inside her. Gabbie went limp in his arms, but he needed to keep her tight to his body in order to feel whole.

They had both exhausted themselves over the evening. Gabbie looked at him and smiled.

"Rock, paper, scissors to see who carries who to bed."

"I'll carry you wherever you want to go," Case said, his baritone voice echoing in the shower.

"I still need to wash my hair," Gabbie said with her eyes hooded from fulfillment.

Case reached with his long arm to the handle, turned on the warm water that cascaded over their bodies. He laid Gabbie back on the tile and covered her with his body.

"Can you stand?"

"Can I? Or do I want to?" Gabbie replied as she stroked Case's bicep and locked her legs around his hips.

"What if I hold you up and wash every inch of your body for you?"

"Has anyone ever died from being spoiled rotten?" Gabbie asked as she kissed Case's darkened lips.

* * * *

Gabbie was exhausted. Every muscle had a good ache in it and it wasn't from the basketball game. It'd been fun to take on Case. She was sure he gave up more baskets then he needed to, but he seemed a little surprised by her three at the end of the game. Either way, being offered to have every inch of her body hand washed by him was something she couldn't turn down, even if she thought the most wonderful feeling in the world was the weight of his body on top of hers.

She was first, always first in his mind it seemed. His long fingers lathered her hair as he lovingly stroked her tongue with his while he washed the soap off under the spray. And he meant it when he said he was going to wash every inch of her body.

What surprised her was he showed the same loving devotion to her shoulder as he did to her breast. There was no extra time spent between her thighs compared to her knee. By the time he was bathing her feet she could have easily been a bubble of soap washing down the drain. She felt treasured and special.

A nagging part of her worried she wouldn't be able to show him the same affection. Gabbie wasn't one to display her feelings outwardly. The outburst on the porch aside, she kept her feelings to herself. But Case seemed, at least when it came to her, to wear his proudly. She wondered if he questioned how much she truly cared for him.

When he had finished, he stood up and Gabbie reached for what looked like his shampoo.

"You take care of enough around here," Case said as he took the bottle from her hand and placed it back on the shelf. "Go to bed, sexy, I'll be there soon."

Chapter Nine

"Biology is the least of what makes someone a mother."
—Oprah Winfrey

"I wanna my mama," Claire screamed on the playground as she held her bloodied knee.

"Claire, it'll be okay. Just let me look at it," Mandy said, trying to calm down Claire's tantrum. She'd been running across the playground in the back of the daycare when she fell down.

"Wants mama Bee Ms. Mand," Claire pleaded.

Normally the staff would try to calm the child down themselves. Even little Lukey knew he wouldn't get Mary Beth if he cried for her. To him all of the owners might as well be his mother. But Mandy was shocked. Initially she thought Claire was asking for her real mom, not Gabbie.

Gabbie was rocking a baby in the infant room while the devastated Claire sat sobbing in the lobby. Mandy came in and shook her head at Gabbie.

"What?"

"Claire wants her mother," Mandy said with her hands on her hips.

"Oh, well…" Gabbie always got a pain her chest when any of the Thomases talked about their parents. It was still so fresh.

"Bee, her mother Bee."

"She called me her mother?" Gabbie said, a little set back.

Claire had said some things over the past few weeks that she was a good mama, but to say she *was* her mama… Gabbie stood up and put the now sleeping Jane in one of the cribs.

In the lobby, Claire sat on the bench by a set of cubbies with her injured leg elevated.

"Mama, I's toreded my preddies," Claire said as her bottom lip trembled.

"I see that," Gabbie said, sitting on her knees in front of Claire and opening the first aid kit Mandy had left on the bench.

"My preddies no more," Claire cried as Gabbie put on latex free gloves and started to clean Claire's injured knee.

The fact she'd hurt herself was not the reason Claire was crying. She had torn her tights or "pretties" as she liked to call them. Claire cherished every one of her pretties. Gabbie had learned Claire was very much a girl, something Gabbie never was. Gabbie never cared about dresses or sparkly shoes when she was growing up, but to Claire they were a necessity.

As Gabbie pulled down Claire's soft pink tights with the lacy backs, Claire looked as if she was being skinned alive. Whatever pain she felt from her scraped knee could have been as great as an amputation, she'd never acknowledge it compared to losing a set of tights to a hole in the knee.

"Mama inks my bess," Claire sobbed as if she was just shot through the heart with an arrow.

"You still have your white and your blue and your orange pretties and don't forget your ones with the little flowers on them."

"I's never gets better preddies..." she declared with all the melodrama befitting Scarlett O'Hara declaring her love for Tara.

"These pretties were almost too small for you since you've been growing so much. How about this?" Gabbie suggested, trying to hold back from laughing in the poor child's face. To Claire this was life or death. "Your daddy and I will pick you up a new pair on the way home and maybe some big girl underwear since you've been doing so good on the potty. These pretties were made for little girls that wear diapers."

Claire's eyes perked up. She started to smile, but only briefly, holding the now-torn tights to her heart as she stood up and stuck her chest out.

"Dees was bestest preddies ever," Claire said as one little crystal tear fell from her dark mahogany left eye, catching on her soft lash then flowing down her chubby cheek.

Gabbie gave Claire a hug to hide the fact she was about to piss her pants from laughing. She released Claire, who returned to the toddler room still clutching her torn tights and Gabbie fell back on the floor and covered her face with her hand so she could laugh without hurting any feelings.

"Is it safe now?" Mandy said holding her gut as she gasped for air. "I lost it when…when she said…" Mandy couldn't hold in her laughter. "I's never gets better pretties. Did you see her lip quivering?"

"She's in pain right now," Gabbie said, trying to be serious. Instead, she ended up rolling on her stomach. "My daughter is such a drama queen."

"Your what?" Mandy said, catching her breath. "Gabbie, she's not your daughter."

"I just called her my daughter," Gabbie sat up and put her head in her hands. What was she thinking?

"Yeah, you and Case have been together a month and you're already claiming children that aren't even his as yours."

"But that's the way he talks. That's the way they all talk. In that house, I'm the mother."

"You don't live in that house, do you?"

Gabbie didn't know how to tell Mandy that Lucy and she had taken up residence.

"Gabbie, what happens if he leaves you?"

Now it was Gabbie who felt like someone had taken her pretties.

"I thought you were happy for me?" Gabbie snapped in self-defense.

"Happy for you if it lasts. It's not like you have a tough skin built up from all your break-ups like I do. And I never fell for kids too," Mandy warned. "What if you start hating Case? You ever think of that? You'll feel trapped because of his kids."

Gabbie could never hate Case, could she? He was tender and loving, said all the right things. He learned he loved kids, and most importantly, loved her.

"I could be their mother," Gabbie said, pushing off the floor. "If nothing else it'll let me treat this as a relationship, not a fling." Gabbie sneered at Mandy who instantly took offense.

Great, now she'd have to make up to Mandy, all because of a damn

81

pair of pretties.

* * * *

"Case, can I see you in my office?" Mr. Clarkson asked.

Case looked at Traun who just shrugged his shoulders.

Mr. Clarkson's office was an eight by eight square that barely fit his desk with a wall full of filing cabinets. Case sat in the steel chair with the dark blue, purple and green upholstery and tried to size up the situation. He was at the end of his internship and Mr. Clarkson was going to have to send off Case's evaluation to his advisor up at UND. Case hoped that was all this was.

"Case, you and Traun have been making great headway with your formulas. I think another six months and you'll have the resealing factor fixed and we could move on to clinical trials."

Case's stomach started to churn with excitement as he swallowed hard. He loved being in control and his output seemed to have gotten him noticed, just like Traun had suspected.

"I need to ask you about Tanya in accounting. Do you know her?"

"We've spoken a few times. I try to avoid her."

"There a reason why?" he asked while shifting his half rimmed glasses to look at a piece of paper in front of him.

"She makes me uncomfortable. I don't like people in my personal space."

"So it's not because you had an affair that went south when she wouldn't forge some expenses you tried to charge to the company?"

Now Case's head spun thinking he'd lose everything because he didn't return that old woman's advances. She clawed at him as if he was raw meat and he was the one getting accused of trying to defraud the company? This couldn't be happening. He needed this job. Without it he could lose the kids and Gabbie. Gabbie—If he was accused of sexual harassment, she'd never forgive him.

Case kept his eyes on Mr. Clarkson. He didn't want to give him one ounce of doubt and to look away could be enough to seal his fate.

"Mr. Clarkson, if you want I have a record at my desk of every overt act that woman made towards me."

"You what?" he asked, taken aback.

"As an intern, I didn't think I had rights, beyond telling her to stop. I was advised by a friend of mine who's an attorney that I should document her actions and my responses. I wasn't looking to get her fired. But if it's between me and her, I need this job and I'm not going to let some woman that can't take a hint destroy everything I've worked for."

"You actually have documentation today?" Mr. Clarkson asked, as relief washed over his face.

"Yes."

"Then it wouldn't be retaliatory," he said with a smile. "That woman has cost this company probably a million dollars in lawsuits and we can't fire her."

"Why did you take her allegation seriously?"

Mr. Clarkson cleared his throat and shifted in his chair.

"The rule in sexual harassment is guilty until proven innocent. I've seen so many guys screwed over," Mr. Clarkson confessed. "Case, you're just starting out. This woman doesn't care who she destroys. Go to your desk and grab your notes. How detailed are they?"

"Very." Case scowled.

"Good, because then she can't say you made it up on the spot."

Case angrily walked to his desk. Tanya passed him in the hallway, a fake smile on her face, and Case had to dig down deep to find the little bit of control he had left in him. Not even calculating the carbon atoms in the shellacked multi-colored monstrosity that was her face could distract him. His fists clenched and he lost it. Punching a cubical wall, he could hear paper and stick pins falling on someone's desk. Thank God it was the end of the day and the person wasn't at their desk.

"Case, baby, are you okay?" he heard Tanya ask from behind him.

He couldn't speak. He couldn't tell the lying bitch he knew what she had done—how she tried to destroy everything in his life, how she didn't care for anyone but herself, how her little games she played to get a few dollars here and there tore apart families and ended careers. All that selfish bitch thought about was herself. He wondered what her children must think of her. They must see her as a wronged victim.

Case got to his desk and unlocked the drawer with his notebook. It was empty. His heart raced as his hand shifted papers around in a desperate search for his salvation. He pulled the drawer out, breaking the rollers as he dumped it on the floor in his cube.

"This what you want?" Tanya asked and he spun to see her holding the black and white composition book in her hands.

"How'd you get that?"

"I've been doing this for years. You think I didn't know what you were scribbling in your little book. Those weren't chemical formulas. I always win."

In Case's mind, he saw Gabbie looking at him with disgust, like she couldn't believe he'd played her. He could see her heart breaking from the lies she'd believe he told. Claire and Charlie screamed for their daddy Ace while being ripped from his arms and placed in his aunt's.

"Your lock was harder than I expected," she smugly said as she leaned against the wall of his cube. "I would have had this shredded before you and Clarkson got done with your little talk."

"Give me that book," Case said and snatched at her as she backed up.

"You take one step towards me and I'll scream like you're beating me. Who you think they'll believe? I've worked here for years and you're just the latest affirmative action intern. The only thing the company will miss is hitting their quotas."

Mr. Clarkson walked around the edge of the cube and snatched the notebook from her fingers. "You know how many years I've looked forward to this, Tanya? I've begged to be reassigned to another area of the building because you can't seem to stop going after my interns."

Tanya stood shocked as Mr. Clarkson leafed through the notes Case had taken.

"Wow, on and off property," Mr. Clarkson said with a smile. "He was just having lunch with his girlfriend and you couldn't help yourself."

"Why her? What does she have?" Tanya snapped. "I'm more of woman than she'll ever be."

"That was last week huh?" Mr. Clarkson said. "Shocking, you placed your formal complaint that afternoon."

"Are you serious?" Case asked, finally feeling free from Tanya's oppressive behavior.

He hadn't comprehended how much he felt as if he was trapped when he came to work until he was vindicated in his beliefs. It hadn't all been in his mind. He had been questioning everything—every interaction, every comment. He'd lost trust in himself. The only place he felt he was a hundred percent right was at home with Gabbie in his arms and the kids playing at his feet.

Case knew he had to make the situation permanent. Beyond adopting the twins, he needed to marry Gabbie. Case had always believed his father was a fool when he talked about love. It felt good to have the security of his parents in love to grow around, but Case thought when he chose a bride it would be his choice. He would control how much of himself he gave to another person. What she'd done on the porch to Madison would have been enough in the past to kick a girl to the curb, but with Gabbie he felt powerless to tell her to kick rocks. There was nothing she could do that was wrong in his eyes and he loved it. The twins would still grow up surrounded by parents they could count on because Case and Gabbie truly loved each other.

"Case?" Mr. Clarkson said and Case came out of his own head.

"Yes."

"You got the job," he said, then looked at Tanya. "If you still want it. It's yours."

"Am I really an affirmative action hire?" Case asked. He'd been vindicated and didn't want to get the job based on his skin color.

"People can call it that," Mr. Clarkson said then placed his hand on Case's shoulder. "But last time I asked a federal law to figure out a chemical formula that will revolutionize the field of medicine, nothing came back. I don't care what color of the person that solves a problem I put out, I hire the human or in this case humans who do it."

"When do I fill out my paperwork?"

"Tomorrow. I have to spend the afternoon in HR with Tanya," Mr. Clarkson said, then leaned in close to Case's ear. "Bitch even delayed your hire date."

Case laughed, then began cleaning up the mess he'd made.

* * * *

Case picked up Chinese and a movie before he got the kids from the center. Gabbie would be stuck there late because she had to close and he stayed with her to clean up.

"What's going on?" she asked when she caught him staring at her.

Claire and Charlie looked at him too. Claire was so happy with her newest pretties they had bought a few nights ago her attention returned to her legs after Case didn't start talking right away.

"Nothing," he said, then got the kids ready to go.

He couldn't help looking at Gabbie. His day had been a rollercoaster of emotions and Gabbie had become the worker who helped him back onto the platform that he could lean on when he couldn't walk straight.

"I got hired full-time, so I don't have to look for a job or new place to live."

Gabbie ran to his arms and hugged him tight.

"I'm so proud of you. You figured out the formula."

"Close enough. They're willing to keep me around to finish it."

"And your partner?"

"Yes. We did everything together."

"That's so great."

"Yeah. I get a real paycheck now."

"Careful. You might become a grown up," she teased while caressing his lips.

Chapter Ten

"Ever notice how 'What the hell' is always the right answer?"
—Marilyn Monroe

The doorbell rang at the center just as Gabbie was moving from her first lesson in the four and five-year-old room to the toddler room. She looked out the full-length glass doors and saw a woman, probably no more than thirty-five, dressed in a designer suit with a man standing behind her.

Something about the woman seemed so familiar, but Gabbie couldn't place it. As she opened the door to greet them, it hit her. This woman looked just like Case's mom did in his high school graduation picture only she had shorter hair that was cut at a sharp angle over her left eye. And her skin was a few shades darker than Case's mom's creamy caramel color.

"Can I help you?" Gabbie asked.

"I'm here to pick up my children," she snapped and pushed past Gabbie. After regaining her balance, Gabbie ran and stepped in front of the woman.

"Excuse me. I know every parent that is allowed to pick up children here. And you aren't one. If you would like to go into my office we can discuss this, but until I know who the hell you are, you aren't stepping one foot near any child here."

The woman looked like the type who always got her way. She reared back as if she was about to snap when the tall gentleman behind her placed his hand on her shoulder.

"This isn't the way, Gwendolyn," he warned.

"Fine, but you'll be added to my lawsuit and possible kidnapping charges."

"My office is this way," Gabbie said, unwavering in her belief that this woman was insane and worse, a danger to every child in her facility.

Once she got the man and woman seated in her office she closed the door and went in search of her partners. Mary Beth was in her office. Mandy had been getting the four and five year olds ready for recess and Sarah was helping feed a baby in the infant room.

"We're on lockdown until I get this woman out of here. She's threatening all sorts of things including kidnapping charges. I'm going to try to not call the police, but Mandy, take the kids out for a long recess. Sarah, you and Jenny lock the door to infant room and Mary Beth, take Tracy and do the same in the toddler room. We're not letting any child out of here until I know who this woman is and what she is thinking."

"Could we really have her kids and not know it?" Mary Beth asked.

"I don't see how. None of our parents told us about a custody battle."

"You sure you can handle this?" Mandy asked.

"I have to," Gabbie said and returned to her office. "I'm sorry about the delay. Can I offer you anything to drink?"

"No," the woman bit. "My name is Gwen Harris. This is my attorney, Marcus Devenshire."

"I'm Gabbie Vaulst, the educational director here. You said we have your children here?" Gabbie asked, thinking, *they only have five sets of siblings in the center and only two sets of African-American ones.*

"Charles and Claire Thomas are my children," she stated plainly and Gabbie might as well have been hit with a knock-out punch by Floyd Mayweather.

"I'm sorry. There must be some mistake. Case Thomas is the guardian of the Thomas twins."

"I'm their mother."

"No, you're not. Their mother..." Gabbie caught herself before saying she was their mother. "...was Marjorie Thomas. She passed away a few months ago."

"But it was my eggs they came from. My sister just carried them. I have court documents stating I can take possession of the twins immediately," she said, flinging a white piece of paper with a blue back at Gabbie.

Gabbie's eyes were clouding over from tears as she tried to make out the muddled type in front of her. Her throat burned as a lump formed the size of Buick, making it hard to breathe.

"This says...you filed a petition," Gabbie said as she went into hyper protective mode.

Claire and Charlie were Case's and hers. She'd never even heard of Gwen Harris and she wasn't about to pass off her babies to a stranger.

"It's signed by a judge. I get partial physical custody..."

"Supervised by her current legal guardian. Which is Case Thomas. Who is not here."

"Of course he's not. A single father has no place raising my children when I could offer them a stay-at-home mother to love and nurture them."

"They're getting a mother who will be with them every day, all day."

Gwen sized Gabbie up. Her eyes seemed to darken before she leaned her forearms on the front of Gabbie's desk.

"So you're the one he's using."

"Using?"

"Did he tell you he loved you?" she snarled through her bright red lips. "I don't see a ring, but I bet he's been saying he'll marry you, hasn't he?"

Gabbie's skin began to crawl listening to this woman bring doubt into every touch Case had ever laid against her flesh.

"Was it fast? Your courtship? Almost surreal? Have you seen the other girls he's dated? Sure, you're pretty with your clear *white* skin," Gwen snipped at the word white as if it caused her physical pain to have her tongue form the word. "Even if he does marry you, there is no way in hell my children are going to be raised by a *white* woman that probably doesn't even know what to do with my daughter's hair."

"You need to leave. Call Case and set up an appropriate time to visit your *niece* and *nephew*. If I see you within fifty feet of my facility without Case I will call the police."

"Try it," she dared, leaning on Gabbie's desk.

* * * *

"Case, you need to come to the center." Gabbie's voice was off. Case could tell.

"Are the kids okay?" he asked, fearing something had happened.

"They're fine. Gwen Harris tried to pick them up today."

"I'll be right there," Case said, hanging up and rushing towards the center.

Now his aunt had gone too far. The judge told her she could have an hour of visitation at Case's home, with him present. Damn those discovery papers saying where he had the kids in daycare.

"This bitch would have never tried this crap at the house with me," Case growled, trying to process the situation. "What the hell makes her think she can just pick up my kids without permission?"

Case hit the hands free phone option on his steering wheel. Rage tore through him at his complete loss of control. Leaving the courtroom, he'd felt empowered. Now he was thanking God that Gabbie was smart enough to not fall for it.

"Call Ron," he spat at the computerized voice.

"Bailey and Howard, this is Stephanie. How can I assist you?"

"Steph, it's Case Thomas. I need to speak to Ron right now."

"I'm sorry, he's with a client right…"

"I don't mean to be an asshole, but the bitch tried to kidnap my children. I need him on the phone now."

"Okay, Mr. Thomas," Steph replied rushed. "I'll see if he can take your call."

Sappy classical musical played throughout the car as Case cut through the side streets to get to his family.

"Case, I got two minutes," Ron said.

"I'll raise your two minutes and give you a psycho. What can we do?"

"First I need to know what happened."

"I got a call from daycare. She tried to take Charlie and Claire."

"How?"

"I don't know. I'm not there yet, but she has no right to do that, does she?"

"No. The judge was clear. If she wasn't willing to submit to the DNA test at a lab of his choosing, he wasn't going to give her anything more than an hour a week. I need a formal statement from your daycare worker. So have her call the local police and file a complaint. Then I can follow up with the judge."

Case pulled into the parking lot of the center right as he hung up the phone. He rushed to the door and punched in his code. Case was met at the door by Mandy, who escorted him to Claire and Charlie.

"Where's Gabbie?" he asked, as he felt relief washing over him, as he looked at Charlie reading a book in the corner and Claire eating an apple at a small table, both ignorant to the fact they were almost ripped from his life.

"She's gone."

"What? Where'd she go? I need her to talk to the cops about what happened."

"I'll talk to the cops. I think she's done enough for you," Mandy sneered.

"What's that supposed to mean?"

"It means your precious aunt laid it all out for her," Mandy said, pulling Case out of the toddler room.

"Laid what out? Mandy you're confusing the hell out of me, and I'm way too stressed to think any deeper than the surface."

"Gabbie hasn't had a man since high school and that jackass was less than pond scum. He hurt her, bad. So learning you were just using her to gain custody will probably end any likelihood she'll ever take a chance on anyone again."

"I'm not using her. I love her."

"That's right, keep up the ruse."

Mandy walked towards the phone at the front desk

"It's not a damn ruse," Case growled and placed his hand over the phone receiver. "I love her. I'm going to marry her. I'm never going to leave her. She's all I want, so tell me where the hell she is."

"She's where she wants to be to get away from you."

"Mandy, I'm going to explain this to you like you're a six-year-old. I want to stop her owie, and her from thinking I was a meany." Case figured the condescending tone might snap Mandy's attitude.

"I knew you were never interested in her. How could you be? Look at you."

"What about me is so detestable?"

"You're somewhere between an eight and a ten…"

"That would be a nine."

"It depends on the day," Mandy snapped. "Gabbie's a six at best. We all knew you were using her."

"You're the one," Case said, looking in Mandy's pathetic eyes. "I always thought it was a guy who made Gabbie so self-conscious about her looks, but it was you."

"I don't know what you're talking about," Mandy snapped as Sarah came out of the infant room to watch the show.

"Gabbie's a goddamn eleven. Unlike you, she has a body. You know…a woman's body, not the body of a ten-year-old boy like you. Men want curves. And her eyes are the most amazing I've ever seen. Maybe it's because of who's behind them, but the way they are so light with the dark eyelashes. She's stunning—without makeup, unlike you who uses spackle. Any woman that needs over a hundred hydrogen atoms per square millimeter of her face to feel presentable to the world—" Case shook his head. "Lose your attitude and you might move up to a four."

Mandy stuttered and stood aghast until Sarah burst out laughing.

"Do you know how long I've wanted to tell her cut the makeup back?"

"Shut up," Mandy snapped.

"Where's Gabbie?" Case asked, again getting back to the matter at hand.

"You love her so much you figure it out."

"The batting cage," Mary Beth said from the door of her office. "The one by highway thirty-six off McKnight. Just realize she's armed and feels betrayed."

Case nodded at Mary Beth in thanks and drove down McKnight to Eleventh St. As he pulled up to the building he reflected on what the protection crew had told him. Gabbie thought he'd been using her all along. He just couldn't understand how she could think that.

Even though it was only one o'clock on a Tuesday the place was still packed. He walked down the aisle hearing the pings as baseballs made contact with bats followed by the subsequent thump as they would hit a wall or net. Occasionally, there was the sound of the ball hitting the gate behind the hitter. At the furthest cage was Gabbie. Her stance leaned back just a bit and wasn't straight on, but didn't seem to affect her swing. He stood at the edge of the cage with his fingers curled around the aluminum gate and watched the beauty of Gabbie's swing.

She had a beat up royal blue batter's helmet on her head and was swinging a metal bat. Still in her work clothes, she looked funny with her cleats on and khakis. He watched her hit ball after ball, not missing one. Case was sure she'd tire soon, but instead of losing momentum, each swing she took seemed to have more power than the last.

Finally, she must have hit the last ball and she flipped the bat in her hands, then dug in her pockets, pulling out another token.

"Gabbie," Case called but she didn't turn. "Gabbie," he said again, this time rattling the cage and she looked at him.

Her beautiful gray eyes were bloodshot and her cheeks were stained from tears she hadn't cared enough to wipe away. Case's anger towards his aunt burned through his whole being as he looked at the pain Gabbie was in.

"Can we talk?" he asked as her fingers hovered over the machine, ready to drop her token.

Biting her upper lip, Gabbie pulled out her earbud from her left ear and looked at him.

"Can we talk?"

"No," she stated plainly, but didn't replace the earbud after she dropped the token.

"Okay, I'll talk, you listen," Case suggested as Gabbie struck the first ball. "I didn't tell you because…I didn't want you to think I was using you to get the kids. I never told my attorney about you. I was trying to win the custody battle on my own, as a single father. I've been dying to ask him how we could adopt the twins together. Call my lawyer if you don't believe me. He'll have no idea who you are."

Gabbie's stance wavered slightly until the third ball came down and she hit it, but it fouled. Case knew she was listening to him now.

"Baby girl, it's okay. I'll keep her away. She'll never take them from us."

"Stop it. Stop acting like there's an us," Gabbie growled, nearly taking the leather off a ball with her hit.

"When we're together, we make love. If I was using you, do you think I'd care about how you'd feel? You've had the other." *Foul ball, good,* Case thought. "I love you, Gabrielle Vaulst. You know that. I've shown that. Don't let some viper come in and take away what we've made."

"She told me about you needing a wife to keep the kids. How you were using me to win a custody battle that you didn't even tell me you were in."

"I should have told you. I take that on myself. But I never wanted you to doubt my feelings for you."

"A single father?" Gabbie asked as she stepped out of the batters box and let the ball slam into the cage. "What if they wouldn't give the kids to a single father?" she asked as she looked at Case.

"I hadn't thought about that. Gwen's been pulling so much shit that my lawyer said it shouldn't be a problem. I swear on my parents' grave I wasn't using you to get the kids."

"I opened the door. What if she uses it against you? I told them about us. Not directly, but I…"

"Didn't do a goddamn thing wrong," Case said, opening the cage and finally taking her in his arms. Since the moment she called he'd felt scared until he felt the comfort of her body against his. "Gabbie I've wanted you since you made that incredible catch in the store, but I couldn't just say that to you because you wouldn't believe how the Thomas men are. Hell, I didn't believe the story my dad told until I saw you."

"What story?"

Case looked at her reddened eyes and frowned.

"Can we get out of the line of fire?" he asked, then guided her out of the cage as the last of the balls flew. "I don't want you to think I'm using you, but my lawyer said you have to file a complaint against my aunt. Can you call the police and make a statement? I didn't want to involve you in this battle."

"You know I'll do anything for the kids," Gabbie said, wringing her

94

hands on the grip of the bat.

"And me?" Case asked as his hands slid around hers and gently pried the *weapon* from her fingers. "What about me?"

"Yet to be determined," she replied.

"Gabbie, I should have told you everything."

"That would've been nice. Why have you never taken me out? In public?"

"We've had lunch."

"You know what I mean."

"I can't afford to until this custody thing is solved. I have a third of my parents' life insurance to live on. I found out once I started my senior year of college they divvied up my trust fund and set up one for the twins instead."

Case wasn't about to tell her he'd been ring shopping on his lunch break, but he understood now how she and all the girls could think he was using her. He wasn't ashamed to be seen with her. He was proud she was with him.

"This is why you've been saving all the receipts and pinching pennies."

"Yes, I can't wait until I get my first paycheck next week and I swear, baby girl, I'll take you anywhere you want to go. I'll tell you everything—everything I should have told you from the start. But before I do, answer my question—when we're making love, do I in any way seem like I'm faking my feelings for you?"

Gabbie looked at him, her eyes finally cleared of tears. The red was still there around her gray irises, but she was starting to calm down. She called for the police, but they said it would be about twenty minutes, so Case slid into a booth with Gabbie and took her hand in his as he traced the inside of her palm.

"You want to hear the story of how my parents met now?"

"Is it going to make me feel better?"

"I hope so. If nothing else, it'll pass the time until the police come," Case said.

He thought back to his father telling him the story when he was young, then again when he was in high school and finally as he helped him pack up for college.

"My father saw my mom across the room at a dance," Case began his story. "My dad said he knew he had to know who she was. He told me there was a spark in him. He didn't know what it was about her—eyes, hair, smile, all of it drew him in. He said it was like a movie where the dance floor parts like the Red Sea and he didn't remember taking a step toward her. Instead it was like he was floating." Case then looked from Gabbie's hand to her eyes and her cheeks blushed red with fire "When he finally got to her, she looked at him like he was crazy. He didn't care. He asked her to dance and they did all night, but she never said a word to him."

"I bet you wished you'd had that from me."

"No," Case said, leaning in closer to her. "Because from the first word my mother said to my father, he knew he'd never love anyone more than her. She told him thanks and left him alone on the dance floor. You said, *you know the no-shopping-cart-theory doesn't work when you have a toddler.*" Gabbie looked at him, surprised he'd remembered the exact words. "I had no idea what you meant, still don't, but your voice…" Case shook his head.

"But you heard me, before you saw me."

"Do you know how incredible it is to know the next person you look at will be the love of your life? Better yet, to turn towards someone whose inner beauty and outer beauty are in constant competition? Gabbie, I loved you before I said it. I loved you before I touched your lips. I loved you before I saw your stunning gray eyes."

Gabbie reached for Case and when their lips met she instantly melted against his body.

"Please don't say it was prom," Gabbie said as she held tight to him.

"What?"

"The dance your parents met at."

"Eighth grade. They had been together for over thirty years when they died. My father died from his injuries. My mother had a concussion and was in and out of consciousness, but it came across the radio they weren't going to transport him. Instead, they declared him dead at the scene. My mother coded a second later. The paramedic said it was broken heart syndrome. He'd seen it before. They said she probably would have been fine, but no matter what they did, they couldn't get her back."

Case wiped away a tear and Gabbie stroked his cheek.

"You still haven't grieved for them have you?"

"When have I had time?"

Gabbie pulled him into her arms and stroked his back as he cried into her shoulder. The last of the ache in his heart disappeared as he finally allowed himself to miss his parents for who they were and not because he needed their help.

Chapter Eleven

"The course of true love never did run smooth."
—William Shakespeare

"Would you tell me about them?" Gabbie asked as she stroked Case's hair, still curled into her chest in the hard plastic booth.

"What do you mean?"

"You've never told me about them besides they loved each other."

"Guess that's the first thing I've always thought about them," Case said with a slight smile, but Gabbie could see tears pooling in his eyes.

A part of her wanted to stop. She didn't want to hear Case's voice crack if he tried to hold back tears. She didn't want to cause him more pain then he was probably already feeling when it came to their loss. But if they were going to make a true life together she needed to be there for him, because from what she'd seen since she met him, he was alone. Gabbie couldn't imagine not having her girls to help her get through hard times. Case's grandparents were so far away from him and now this woman had come and threatened his children.

Right as he was about to speak, Gabbie saw a police officer step through the door. Sighing, she placed her hand on Case's knee and prepared herself for her statement.

"Ms. Vaulst?" the tall blond officer asked as he approached.

"Yes."

"I was just with Amanda at Growing Strong. She indicated you were the one that did most of the talking with the suspect."

"Yes, I was. Please sit."

As Gabbie replayed the situation, Case's arm slipped behind Gabbie and he squeezed her tighter to his body. The warmth and security kept her focused on the task at hand—keeping the twins safe. As they were wrapping up, the officer went over where Case was legally with his aunt, and Gabbie felt Case's thumb go under the bottom of her shirt. It stroked her spine and slid under the top of her waistband, then up again. Case did all this with a cool, calm control as he spoke to Officer Hansen about all that had happened since the loss of his parents.

Gabbie saw Case's jaw become a hard line as he sucked in his lips and bit on them. She placed her hand on his thigh and he looked at her as if the contact was a shock to him. Pulling his hand from behind her, she realized he hadn't noticed his stroking thumb. It had been an involuntary action on his part.

When the officer left, Gabbie turned to Case, unsure of what was going to happen next. She couldn't even remember where they had left off. She could only remember he was curled into her chest, crying.

"Now what?" Gabbie asked as her fingers played with the card the officer had left by pressing it against the pads of her fingers as she rotated it on its sides.

"You still want to know about my parents?"

"Of course. Why would I not?"

"I don't know. It's just…"

"Hard for you."

"Yeah, but I think you would have liked them. My father worked as an assistant in my lawyer's office while he went to night school. My mom worked at Target during the day and on weekends. Grandma helped raise me until I was about seven when my father had finally finished getting his law degree. After a year working as a lawyer, he made my mom quit working."

"You got to have your mom there a lot growing up?"

"Yeah, not that I appreciated it. I was a little shit. All I wanted was my dad, but he worked late to give us everything he could."

"It seemed to have worked."

"I am grateful. My mom was the one who kept the money in order. Her parents didn't believe in credit. You want a car, you pay in full."

"I thought that only worked on beaters."

"Would you believe the car I'm driving now was my parents' first car that wasn't six years old at least?"

"No," Gabbie said nuzzling against his neck.

The musky smell of his cologne slipped into her lungs. The warmth of his arms took away the chill that came in from the door that had been opened around the corner. Case lifted his left arm and checked his watch.

Gabbie wanted to be alone with him. He was right. They didn't just have sex. As much passion as they had, there was something there when he stroked her thigh, or when he let his thumb glide across her lip.

Gabbie looked up at Case and saw he'd lost the sadness and stress from his eyes. If she hadn't already noticed his hand had unconsciously started to squeeze her ass, the hooded desire and lip biting of Case told her everything she needed to know. She was turning him on even though a part of him was fighting it.

"You know I don't have to go back to work. The girls will expect me to be gone for the rest of the day," Gabbie said as she inched out of the booth with Case's hand in hers.

"I told my boss I wasn't sure how long I'd be in court today," Case added as he took the lead, practically pulling Gabbie's arm out of the socket to get her to the parking lot.

"I'll only do this if you're using me for my body," Gabbie said.

Case wrapped her up in his arms and growled against her ear. "Gabrielle, I'm going to show you how to use your body."

"I don't want to do it alone," Gabbie teased as she felt him harden.

"Fuck your toes, I'm going to make your hair curl."

"You have such sexy pillow talk," Gabbie said, then slid her hand in his pocket, pulling out his keys. "First one there gets to pick the room," she said as she tossed his keys across the parking lot.

"Cheater."

Gabbie jumped in her car and turned it over, still careful to not run over Case who was racing across the concrete to retrieve his keys.

* * * *

There are those people that are family and those that are friends. Either can become the other. For Gabbie, no matter the situation, Mary

100

Beth, Mandy and Sarah were her sisters. Although they fought and had different opinions at times, they still would kill for each other…that is, if they didn't kill each other first.

Gabbie was curled up in Case's arms, watching a movie with the twins happily building towers with wood blocks on the carpet in front of the couch. The doorbell rang and a chill shot through Gabbie's body. The fear that Gwen was on the other side of that door coming to disrupt the calm night she and Case had finally come to, was almost too much for her to bear.

Case could feel the tension cut across Gabbie's body and he gave her a tight squeeze.

"I'll get it, baby girl," he said as he kissed the top of her head.

Gabbie felt cold when the heat of Case's body wasn't there to protect her. Looking down at Claire and Charlie playing, she prayed that one of them would need a hug at that moment. She didn't want to stop their play, but she really wanted to hold on to at least one of the Thomases at that moment. Charlie, the most sensitive of all the Thomas', must have sensed her tension and left the blocks to climb up on the couch to lie on Gabbie's lap.

With her arms wrapped around Charlie, she felt right again. Case walked back in the room with Mandy in tow. She didn't seem like herself; her head was down and her hands were wringing.

"What happened?" Gabbie asked. Mandy was never upset.

Gabbie stood up with Charlie on her hip and walked to Mandy, who put on a fake smile for Charlie. She booped his nose with her finger and he giggled a little, but even he knew something was wrong.

"Come here, Lil' Man," Case said, taking Charlie in his arms, but Charlie clung to Gabbie. "I need to give Claire a bath and I don't want you to even try to get in the water."

Of course, Claire had already knocked over the blocks in her sprint to the bathroom after hearing the magic word.

"Mama's okay, Charlie," Gabbie said.

Charlie finally released his death grip and went to Case, who leaned into Gabbie's ear and kissed her as he whispered, "I love your beautiful self."

She wasn't sure why he said it that way. Even Case had a different vibe now.

"I'll give you two some privacy," he said, as he walked to the bathroom where Claire was already complaining about no water and bubbles.

"What's going on?" Gabbie asked as she and Mandy sat on the couch.

Mandy fiddled with her fingernails and kept swallowing hard. Gabbie could see tears pooling in Mandy's eyes. Mandy never cried. Not once that Gabbie had ever seen.

"Sometimes I'm not nice…" Mandy's voice was raspy. "I don't mean to be. I'm surprised you'd even allow me in here after…" the words caught in Mandy's throat.

"After what?"

"What I said at work today."

"What did you say?"

"Case didn't tell you?"

"Nope."

"I said he was using you and we all knew it because you were a six at best."

"Six?" Gabbie felt as if she'd been slapped across the face. Now she understood Case's comment. She hadn't felt like a six since she met Case.

"You know I love you, but I couldn't see…"

"How he could?"

"Yeah."

"Because I'm so…"

"Gabbie don't. I was sticking up for you."

"Sticking up for me! Is that 'cause I'm too ugly to do it for myself…am I stupid too?"

The day had taken its toll on Gabbie's nerves. She had almost lost her children and thought that she had been taken advantage of by her lover. The last thing she needed was her supposed best friend describing how calling her ugly and useless was in her best interests. This was not the way she wanted to end the day. Gabbie was never one to cry when attacked, but she was one to fight.

"No," Mandy pleaded as she held Gabbie's hands, before Gabbie ripped them away.

"Funny," Gabbie said, getting up and crossing to the window. "Case didn't say a thing to me, probably because he didn't want to hurt me. I could have gone my whole life and been happy to not know you thought I belonged ringing a bell tower."

"I didn't say you were Quasimodo. I just thought that he's…gorgeous."

"You're the only one that deserves a hot guy. I got you. Any other nuggets you wish to impart on me?"

"I'm a bitch."

"Already common knowledge," Gabbie said as she turned towards Mandy. "We know you're a bitch. We deal with it because we all know how fragile you are."

"I'm not fragile."

"Bullshit," Gabbie barked as both their voices rose. "One bad look from a guy and you go all defensive as if his opinion is all that matters. And if a girl doesn't find you the hottest thing since sliced bread…"

"I am the hottest thing since sliced bread," Mandy snapped as they started to circle each other.

"The only hot thing on you is your snatch that you put out there for everyone. You know your nickname is fire crotch…that name's usually reserved for the red heads. How'd you earn it?"

"Just because people want mine—"

"Most people pick up free samples when they're handed out on the corner. They rarely buy though. Most get tossed in the trash."

Mandy shoved Gabbie who pushed back and then pinned Mandy underneath her on the couch. A myriad of *you bitch, slut, whore* and *I hate yous* poured out of them at a record pace. They both pinched and pulled hair in an effort to right themselves, but Gabbie kept the upper hand.

"Let go, Vaulst, or I swear I'll bite your arm," Mandy growled, unable to move from Gabbie's death grip around her neck.

"You bite my arm and you'll be eating elbow, bitch," Gabbie warned as she yanked Mandy's hair back.

"You don't even know what to do with a man."

"I hate you so much," Gabbie growled as she wrenched Mandy's arm behind her back. "I'm allowed an orgasm, too, you whore."

"And that kids, is how not to behave," Case said and the women locked in battle turned toward his voice to see Claire and Charlie staring. "They wanted to give mama a kiss goodnight. Mandy, could you let go of Gabbie's hair so she can give them a goodnight hug and kiss?"

Mandy and Gabbie both released their holds on each other. Gabbie smoothed out her hair and clothes as she tried to calm herself, hoping to rid the red flush from her face to no avail. Her heart was beating like a stampede of mustangs were running through her chest. Bending down on her knees, she felt the bruise already starting to form from where Mandy had kicked her.

"What's a gasam, Daddy?" Claire innocently asked.

Case looked down at her. Gabbie and Mandy both covered their smiling lips.

"Something daddies give mommies when they're good and, obviously, Momma had too many today."

Gabbie couldn't believe Case's candid comment about their afternoon adventures.

"Oh…Mama naughy. Mama gives Daddy back his gasam."

Mandy had to turn around at that point as Gabbie and Case locked eyes, each daring the other to not laugh.

"Mama was being naughty. Even mamas make mistakes, but I'll see what I can do."

"Mama, yous and Miss Mand funny," Claire said as she hugged Gabbie.

"Yous gots to say sorry Miss Mand, Mama," Charlie said as he gave her a hug.

"I will say I'm sorry, I promise," Gabbie said as she stood up to see Case biting his lips to stop from laughing.

"I'm a little offended," he said as Gabbie tried to avoid his eyes. "Am I just an orgasm to you?"

"No, oh my god," Gabbie said, covering her face with her hands.

Case wrapped his arms around her and she wanted to cry, but couldn't figure out what to do between the laughing embarrassment.

"I'd hate to see what you did to the refs when you played ball," he said, then leaned in closer to her ear. "Save that energy for the bedroom, please."

"I don't think I'll be able to move for the next week," she replied, still shaking from the fight.

"I think you needed this release. It's been a hard day, and I prefer that you take it out on anyone but me," Case said, then looked at Mandy on the couch and nodded. "Amanda."

"Night, Case."

Gabbie gave Case a goodnight kiss since that's what the kids wanted to see every night. As Case walked the twins to their room, Mandy got up and hugged Gabbie from behind and rested her chin on her shoulder.

"You know how jealous I am of you?" Mandy asked. Gabbie patted Mandy's head.

"You've always been jealous 'cause you didn't have my ass."

"Ice cream?"

"I got pistachio."

"This is your house, isn't it?" Mandy teased as they walked into the kitchen.

Gabbie set out two bowls and got the pistachio ice cream and requisite chocolate syrup for Mandy. They'd fought before—called each other everything but the son of God. Gabbie was sure that day was coming eventually.

"I was sticking up for you at first," Mandy explained as she drizzled the chocolate over her ice cream then wiped the cap with her finger to catch any missing drops.

"I'm sure."

"I was," Mandy said emphatically. "Come on, you know what you thought when you left. What did he say to you?"

"That he loved me and I believed him." Gabbie put a spoonful of ice cream in her mouth then looked down. "Do you believe in love at first sight?"

"I fall in love every night."

"No, you don't," Gabbie said as she shifted on the stool at the island. "Have you ever seen someone and thought he's the one with just one look?"

"That how you feel about Case?" Mandy asked.

"He said that's how he feels about me."

"Honest?" Mandy asked and Gabbie could see the confusion in Mandy's hazel eyes. "I didn't mean it to sound that way. I swear I don't mean…"

"To be a bitch," Gabbie kidded. "It's your face."

"What's wrong with my face?"

"Your nose is a little too small…" Gabbie snickered. "Here's the deal. You can't make your face and voice match."

"What am I doing wrong?"

"'Cause I know and love you I know you're sincere. It's…just…your voice sounds condescending and your face is all scrunched like I did something wrong."

"That's not what I mean."

"I know. You're honest and you have my back. I'm sure if Case had been lying to me you'd have helped me bury the body."

"A rational man would get a restraining order on your ass," Case said as he snuck in the kitchen and snatched Gabbie's ice cream from her. "Are you two good again?"

"Always," Gabbie said, smiling at Mandy, who true to form had a face that seemed uncertain even though Gabbie knew Mandy was all right too.

"This happen a lot between you guys?" Case asked as he balanced the spoon between his teeth.

"Depends… Are you asking for a restraining order?" Gabbie teased as she raised her right eyebrow.

Case pressed against Gabbie's body, essentially trapping her between his arms.

"I like that you can't be restrained," he growled against her neck. "Don't you owe me something?"

Gabbie's body flushed. She looked at Mandy who shook her head. The look on Mandy's face could be construed as vile hate, but Gabbie knew better. Mandy was jealous Gabbie was moving on, not that Gabbie had found someone who loved her.

Case pushed back and leaned against the counter across from the island. He finished what was left in her bowl, but fed her as he did. Gabbie hadn't put a double helping in like she usually did when they curled up on the couch to eat ice cream together. Case added another two scoops to the bowl and Gabbie smiled, thinking about all the traditions they had started since she had sort of moved in. Maybe it was time to get rid of her apartment permanently.

Case seemed sure they'd be a family. Claire and Charlie wouldn't go to bed until they saw 'mommy and daddy' kiss goodnight. Case couldn't get comfortable on the couch until she came home at night and she was lying in his arms.

Whether their family was formed in a flash or over ten years, Gabbie knew it didn't matter. They were a family and if Case would let her, she was going to help fight for their children.

Chapter Twelve

"If you want your children to be brilliant, read them fairy tales. If you want them to be geniuses, read them more fairy tales."
—*Albert Einstein*

Gabbie had been right. Case did owe her a night out, just the two of them. Even if it was something as simple as eating subs then going to get groceries after, he was sure he could turn the simple into something wonderful. When he arrived at Growing Strong, he walked straight to Gabbie's office. He'd already secured Mandy as a babysitter so he scooped Gabbie off her chair and into his arms.

"What are you doing?"

"I'm pickin' up my lady," he stated and walked her out of the center.

"What about your kids?"

"*Our* kids are going to be just fine. Adult supervision has been procured," he informed her as he set her down and opened the door to his car.

"What about my keys? I'll need my car."

"Why? You have a guy willing to drive you around the city and no need for a car until tomorrow afternoon."

"My phone," she said with her arms crossed.

"I don't want the distraction." He ran his fingers through her hair and cradled her head in his hand. "You're mine tonight."

"This is that romance thing you promised me, huh?"

"You up for it?"

Gabbie stroked her thumb across Case's bottom lip and he nipped at it. Rising to her tip-toes, her soft lips touched his and he returned with a light lick to hers.

"Take this slow. Romance is only in movies."

"That explains the cameras around us right now." He smiled down into her soft gray eyes and a blush crossed her cheeks.

Sliding into the driver's seat he turned to Gabbie.

"Romance is what you make of it, you know that right?"

"You're being ominous again, Guardian."

His hand curled around hers as he placed them both on his leg.

"I don't ever want to disappoint you."

"I think I've told you plainly when you've screwed up. Don't set yourself up for failure. Romance me."

"Yes ma'am." Case pulled out of the parking lot and drove them to the Woodbury library.

"Okay?" Gabbie looked at him with a cocked eyebrow.

"You trust me?"

"Yes. I didn't know you were going to bring me to the library... Are you going to read me sonnets from a dead poet?"

"No," Case said then reached in the backseat for his backpack. "You know I like when you're naughty right?"

Gabbie's face flushed a bright fire engine red at that comment.

"Are we going to make-out in the how-to section?"

"No."

* * * *

Case got out and opened Gabbie's door for her. Locking his arm around hers he escorted her into the library. Gabbie hadn't been in a public library since she was in grade school. She preferred to use the school's library—something about it being part of her tuition that paid for it being the main motivator.

The Woodbury library didn't slouch on the greenery. There was a man-made waterfall and a path that had tall and flowing ferns and other trailing plants. Case walked her to the full-length glass wall and they sat on a U shaped bench. He placed his backpack in between the two of them and smiled at her.

The worn navy blue bag was tattered and the tough nylon outer fiber was frayed slightly by the leather bottom. Gabbie's left eyebrow arched as she watched him unpack the two subs, pickles and two twenty-ounce pops. The checkered receiving blanket he'd found still in its package when he cleaned the twin's closet served as a great 'blanket' on their bench. The sun had started to set outside, but with east facing windows they got the remnants of the pinks and purples.

"Part of the reason I don't take you out is because I don't want to share you," he explained. Twisting the top off her pop, Case continued. "I already have to share you with *our* two beautiful children that you didn't have to go through a second of labor with…" Gabbie blushed and unwrapped the paper surrounding her sandwich. "But you seem to have a set of sisters that need you and finally, I know you have to finish school."

Gabbie was going to say something, then held her tongue. Listening to all Case had to say and knowing that it was important to hear his words, she wasn't going to protest.

"More importantly, I don't take you out because I don't want to get arrested."

"Arrested?"

Case placed his hand on Gabbie's knee then slowly slid it up her thigh. With a light squeeze he leaned over and softly placed a kiss on her lips.

"When I'm around you it's very hard to not strip you down and see if I can get your eyes to roll back in your head."

Gabbie shifted feeling the shameful wetness pooling underneath her.

"You like that?"

"The only thing I don't like is I don't get to look in your beautiful eyes."

"Two days in a row. Case, I'm going to think you like me."

"I think we're way past two days, Gabbie."

"The sweet talk. You're going to give me a cavity soon."

"I'm making up for lost time."

"You only made me wait for two weeks," Gabbie said and took a small bite of her sandwich. "And you've more than made up for that little transgression."

"Two weeks? Not me. I'm making up for all the years you waited for me to come into your life. It drives me crazy that we lived ten minutes apart and never crossed paths."

"You played indoors and I played outdoors."

Case smiled. "Yet here we are, surrounded by the outdoors, inside."

"You're not that good," Gabbie said. There was no way that he had actually thought that through when he planned this date.

"You'll never know and I'll never tell."

Gabbie had to smile at his playful attitude. He had made a romantic moment in the most unconventional of places.

"It's about the experience, Gabbie, not the expense. Sorry I took so long to figure that out. You wanna dance?"

"Dance?"

"Yeah."

Case stood up and pulled out his phone. Gabbie took his outstretched hand with a smirk. He pulled her into his arms. His chest was firm and strong against her cheek. A long finger slid under her chin and raised her eyes to his. Slowly he placed an ear bud in Gabbie's ear. She shivered when his finger tickled her ear lobe then twisted her hair.

Placing the other ear bud in his ear he caressed her lips as the music started to play *2 Occasions,* by Babyface, in her right ear. Case leaned down so his cheek brushed against hers.

With his right hand on the small of her back and his left hand encircled hers, they rocked in a circle. The warmth of his breath tickled her neck. Gabbie wrapped her left hand around his strong shoulder and held on, their private concert playing just to them. She stayed on her tiptoes to avoid losing the connection. Gabbie wanted him as close as he could be.

The spicy sport smell of his cologne mixed in her nose. Case was better than the few flowers that surrounded them. He was what she always wanted in her life—the warmth, the love, the romance. She flashed to their first kiss—the monumental event that had left her shaking, trying to remember how legs held a body upright.

Case released her hand and let his right hand glide down her back. She curled her fingers into the mauve cotton polo he was wearing that day. How could she ever measure up to this person he thought she was? The thought scared her and she clung tighter. She knew she wanted to be with him, but she didn't want to be a drain on him. *Stop it*, she told herself. *He loves you and you love him. He'll give you the world and you'll do the same.*

"You okay there, Baby Girl?"

"Yes," Gabbie said into his chest. Her voice hitched. "I just love you."

"Glad I'm not the only one."

"Never."

"You ready for the second part of the date?"

"There's more?"

"We need to get groceries…we're almost on E."

"And…" Gabbie started to make a snippy comment about getting groceries being a date, but stopped herself. Never in a million years would she have ever thought going to the library could be romantic and she was on the verge of tears, unable to understand the emotions running through her at that moment. Instead, she passed Case his ear bud and said, "Lead on."

* * * *

Dancing hadn't been on the agenda, but it was the perfect surprise topper to the meal. Now Case had to figure out how to turn a trip to *Cub* into something that would have her smiling to herself when she sat at her desk tomorrow.

"Okay. We're on a mission."

"A mission?" Gabbie echoed with a sparkle in her eyes.

Case loved the way the bridge of her nose would wrinkle up when she was being fun. Challenging her seemed to bring out the kid in her that had been lost when she and her friends grew up at eighteen and became business owners instead of college students. Gabbie was the mom of the group, always taking care of others—her dad, the girls, the kids at the center. Case had decided that she was not going to be his caretaker; he was going to let her have fun and take care of her forever.

"Don't laugh…actually I love your laugh… Just don't laugh at me," Case said as he remembered the best sound in the world was Gabbie, Claire, and Charlie giggling when they were chasing through a pillow fort they had built last weekend.

"Got it."

"You sure? Because I'm not even sure what I just said."

"I speak two-year-old, remember?"

"Right," Case replied as he pulled out an envelope as if he was secret agent. "In here we have coupons."

"Coupons…you…" Gabbie giggled then sat straight up as if ready to receive her orders. "Continue."

"We are going to coupon shop. Your mission…"

"Should I choose to accept it…"

"Exactly."

Case loved the way they played together. Gabbie wasn't just the love of his life. She was the best friend he'd ever had. He kept the serious straight-forward tone and Gabbie was more than happy to play along.

"Only buy items with a coupon."

"What if we *need* something that we don't have a coupon for? Like bread."

"Find a coupon or we will eat crackers."

"Crackers? Got it."

"This is Hell's Impossible Iron Top Chef Woodbury edition. You have to save money and feed a family of four and a half or risk being chopped."

"A half?"

"Lucy's low on cat food."

"Whew," Gabbie sighed as if exhausted by the mission in front of her.

"Do you accept this mission?"

"How much time do we have to complete it?"

Case looked at his watch, then to Gabbie, then back at his watch. Doing this fast could be fun. Going with his gut, he decided on a time frame.

"Working together we have forty-five minutes to be in the check-out line."

"I will accept your mission."

"Time starts…" Case looked at Gabbie, whose hand was curled around her door handle. He loved when she was competitive. "Now."

They both took off towards the store, catching each other's hands as they walked through the automatic sliding glass doors. Case went for the cart as Gabbie grabbed the store flyer and started to scan the coupons.

The 'mission' started out as joke and quickly escalated into an all-out challenge for superiority. Case was going for speed and Gabbie handled efficiency by sifting through the coupons while Case was grabbing two bags of potatoes that were buy one get one free. By the time he had them in the cart, Gabbie had not only found what they actually needed—she had it separated by aisle.

Case and Gabbie tag teamed up and down the aisle timing each other to see who could grab what quicker.

"Faster Vaulst," Case goaded.

"I was a stationary player thank you very much. And you only needed one thing last aisle. So not fair."

She argued as she ran to the cart dropping the items into the basket.

"Not my fault you got the canned aisle and I got the jelly one."

By the time they got to paper goods they were both panting and laughing. Case had Gabbie wrapped in his arms as he dipped his head down to hers.

"Wait," she said frantically. "Time?"

Case had forgotten the game five aisles ago, but loved that Gabbie hadn't quit.

"Um…" Case looked at his watch. "Oh crap. We got two minutes to be in line."

Case pushed the cart as Gabbie sprinted to get a place in line. When he caught up with her she started to unload the cart, but he stopped her. Taking her in his arms he kissed her. Her soft body conformed to his in a way that made him realize he probably shouldn't have started this. He was stiffening and could feel himself digging into her hip.

"Don't make them call the cops," Gabbie said breathless against his lips.

"Can we finish this in the car?"

"Car…garage…kitchen…hallway…you play your cards right… we'll make it to bed."

"I'll bag."

Chapter Thirteen

"No one can make you feel inferior without your consent."
—Eleanor Roosevelt

The home phone rang, catching Gabbie off guard. She walked around the kitchen then followed the ring of the phone into the living room.

"Hello?"

"Who's this?" an older woman asked.

"Gabbie."

"Is Case Thomas there?"

"He's not home from work yet. Can I take a message?"

"Oh, this is just his nana," she said. For some reason Gabbie straightened up her back and smoothed her shirt. "Tell him I need to know if he'll be picking his papa and me up at the airport on Friday or if we'll need to get a car."

"This weekend?"

"He'll know what I'm talking about."

"Okay ma'am, I'll let him know."

After hanging up Gabbie couldn't help but wonder what was going on. The fact that his grandma didn't register her name also dug into her. Then she remembered she probably should call her dad and let him know she was living with a guy. She tried not to be distracted while she cooked, but she ended up burning the rice.

"What's burning?" Case asked as he walked in from the garage.

"Oh God," Gabbie exclaimed, running back into the kitchen and tossing the pot into the sink.

Her hands covered her face out of embarrassment and then the negative thoughts that had been screaming in her head for the last half hour snapped.

"What's this weekend?"

"The twelfth I think?" Case replied with an uneasy tone.

"And?"

"And I'm confused."

"Your grandma called. She wanted to know if you'd be picking her up from the airport."

"What airport?"

"The one with the planes. I don't know."

"Why are you mad?"

"Because… I want to be."

Case circled the island in the middle of kitchen then came to the sink. He looked at Gabbie and she got more upset because all she wanted was her honey-I'm-home-kiss. Biting her bottom lip, she stood with her arms crossed and turned her eyes away.

"I'm going to call my grandma and find out why she's coming here. You're going to give me a better answer when I come back."

Gabbie didn't have a better answer. She followed Case into the living room and rested against the doorjamb between the two rooms, determined to hear at least half the story.

"Nana, it's Case… That's this weekend? I wasn't even planning on going up… I know, but…" Case turned, saw Gabbie and waved her over to him. "I gotta check with my girlfriend. Yes, that's who answered the phone…" Case wrapped his arm around Gabbie's waist and every ounce of anger dissipated. "Gabbie, my graduation is in Grand Forks this weekend. I wasn't planning to go, but my grandparents bought their tickets in January. So do you think you could go?"

"Of course. The kids will be a challenge but we'll get 'em up there."

"Kids," Case said shaking his head. "Right…um…" Case turned back to the phone. "Nana I'm going to have to—"

Gabbie covered the receiver and stopped Case.

"They have to get a car because we only have a five passenger vehicle. Don't let Claire and Charlie miss out on their grandparents."

"Nana you'll have to get a car. We don't have enough seatbelts with the twins. I don't know which hotel we're staying at, but that sounds like a nice one. I'll see you there on Saturday morning… I love you too. Yes, she'll have the kids with her. Bye, Nana."

Case hung up and sighed.

"Now I gotta see if I can still be part of the graduation," he said as he pulled out his cell phone and dialed. "You have a better answer to why you were mad?"

"Because I'm an idiot."

"Fine. When's dinner going to be ready?"

"After I remake the rice."

Gabbie looked at the stressed-out Case and felt guilty for being so upset. He'd been so caught up in their crazy life he'd forgotten about his own. With the help of his coach, Case was able to acquire last minute tickets to his graduation ceremony and ordered his gown. All the final preparations had been made and Gabbie switched days off so they could leave first thing Friday morning.

* * * *

Case had somehow gotten the last room in the city, and it wasn't at a sleazy no-tell-motel, but instead a nice chain hotel. His grandparents checked in with Case when they landed. Tired from the trip, they said they'd meet everyone for breakfast.

With the kids asleep in one of the queen size beds, Gabbie and Case settled in under the covers. Resting on her forearm, Gabbie kissed an exhausted Case and smiled.

"You're graduating tomorrow."

"Uh huh."

"Are you okay?"

"Just tired, this week's been stressful."

"I'm proud of you."

"Are you?"

"I think we need to do something just for you."

"I can think of something," Case growled as he stroked back a few loose strands of Gabbie's hair and cupped the back of her head. Gently, he pulled her toward him so he could kiss her lips.

"I bet you could."

"You'd be under the covers, they'd never know."

"You're serious?" Gabbie chuckled.

"Not really, unless you're up for it."

"If it's what you want, but I was thinking about we put money aside and let you take a vacation."

"Maybe," Case said as he wrapped his arms around Gabbie and pulled her to his chest. "You coming with me?"

"I thought it was supposed to relax you."

"If you're in my arms I feel peace."

"Then I'll bite the bullet and suffer through a vacation with you."

"White sandy beaches?"

"Mmmmm."

"Palm trees."

"Sounding good."

"Private hut with side by side massages."

"And every night…"

"I keep you up until sunrise. Tonight," Case growled and brushed back Gabbie's hair.

"Charlie and Claire are five feet away," Gabbie whispered.

"And dead to the world. I'll be quick," Case said crawling on top of Gabbie and falling between her legs. "Fifty pumps. Count 'em if you're bored."

"With an offer like that..." Gabbie giggled. "Seriously, Case…oh, my God."

Case began brushing his lips against her neck and Gabbie bit down on hers to keep in the moan that was building. She could feel he wasn't kidding about needing a release. The hardness pressing against her was more of a tease than his lips.

"Baby," he moaned.

"What is going on?"

"I don't know. Something about being back in Grand Forks… It's like when I had a roommate…"

"I don't want to hear about your other women."

"How about I tell you about my hottest woman?"

"Hmm."

"Do you know how gorgeous you looked when you were reading *The Going to Bed Book*. The way you smile when you talk about pajamas. I never understood the whole sexy mother of my children thing…but you are the sexiest…" Case nibbled on Gabbie's ear. "Alluring…" His hand traveled from Gabbie's hip to her breast which he gently massaged. "Delicious…Oh god, Gabbie, please…" He caressed Gabbie's lips in such a way she couldn't help but pull the covers over their heads.

"If the bed squeaks once…" she warned, holding up her finger.

"God I love you," Case said as he guided himself inside her.

The soft, quiet lovemaking had Gabbie shaking against Case's every touch. Their mouths stayed fused to keep the moans to a minimum. The fifty-stroke promise was forgotten as they both ground against each other to avoid the bed making any noise.

After they both climaxed, Gabbie poked her head out from the cover and checked on the kids who were, true to form, oblivious in their slumber. Case kissed the top of Gabbie's head and they both drifted into peaceful slumber. They woke, unfortunately, too early with a cannonball from the squealing duo.

"That's it," Case grumbled as he body slammed Charlie to the bed and started Ticklefest 2012.

After everyone was cleaned up, they all went to meet Case's grandparents.

"There's my babies," Nana said as Charlie and Claire ran to her.

"Nana," they both sang as they wrapped their arms around her neck.

Case kept his hand on Gabbie's back as he escorted her through the tables of the restaurant. Gabbie held tight to Case as his grandpa stood up and extended his hand.

"You must be Gabbie," he said. "I'm Case's Papa Teddy."

"Nice to meet you."

"Mama," Claire said, taking Gabbie's hand and bringing her to the table. "Mama yous sits by mes."

"Mama?" Nana said looking at Case. "Did that child just call her mama?"

"Dis mys Mama Bee, Nana," Claire said without hesitation. "She's a good mama. She makeses the bestest fasts for us."

"I'm glad to hear that, baby. Case is this woman making breakfast at your house?"

"Nana, Papa Teddy, Gabbie's very special to us all."

"Oh lord, where have we heard this before," Papa Teddy said shaking his head. "He's just like his damn daddy."

"I hope so," Case said. "I hope I'm as lucky as him."

"Gabbie, I need you to sit between me and Claire. Let's keep the womenfolk together."

Gabbie sat between Nana and Claire and tried not to fidget. After the food was served and Case and Papa Teddy were distracted, Nana turned to Gabbie.

"You're the one who convinced my Case he needed to keep his family together,"

"It wasn't that hard," Gabbie admitted. "He has a strong sense of family."

"I'm glad he was payin' attention growing up, but I have to worry about you."

Gabbie felt a kick to her gut. She'd feared being unwanted and an outsider. She feared that she'd lose the place she'd made in the family if what was left of Case's family disapproved of her.

"I never thought I'd be the one askin' this question, but what are your intentions when it comes to my grandchildren?"

"Um…well…" Gabbie knew what she and Case had talked about. Although he hadn't asked her directly, she felt in her heart that one day he would marry her, and as she looked at Case across the table, he winked and gave a knowing smile. "I'm hoping to someday marry one and mother two."

"You sure about that? That's a big responsibility to take on when they aren't your children."

"Where a child comes from doesn't determine their importance in my life," Gabbie said as she started to cut up Claire's sausage into bite size pieces.

"Mama," Claire scolded. "I's big."

"Oh are you?" Nana asked with a raised eyebrow.

"Mama's taughted me."

"You're right, Claire, you can cut your own sausage, but remember what to do when you need to say something and adults are talking."

"Sorry, Mama. I forgots."

"It's okay. It's a crazy day. Here you go." Gabbie passed Claire the butter knife to cut. Nana watched in fascination as Claire used her fork and knife to cut her own sausage. It was messy but she got it done and smiled with pride as she ate.

"I'm blessed to have helped over a hundred children grow up over the last few years, but none have made me happier than Claire and Charlie. I love them and would do anything to protect them."

"How long have you and Case been together?"

"Not long enough. That I know, but there's something about him and the way we are together. All of us."

"What if he doesn't feel the same?"

"Then he shouldn't have moved me in, because I love Claire and Charlie so much. I'd do anything for them and I can't imagine not having them in my life."

"Guess that's why Claire says you're a good mama then," Nana said. "Case has too much of his father in him. Don't let it scare you away."

"That's not where my fear lies."

"Where does it lie?"

"It's just been fast."

"Thomas men don't know how to take anything slow," she said shaking her head. "I learned that with my daughter, but they are a faithful loving lot."

"Yes, they are," Gabbie replied with a smile.

"He looks happier than I've seen him in years."

"I know I'm the happiest I've ever been."

"Then everything is right with the world, even if the world ain't right."

"I am sorry about your daughter and son-in-law. They seemed like amazing people."

"They were and never in a million years did I think they'd beat me to the grave, but between you and Case at least I know my babies here will be raised right."

Gabbie held in her questions about Aunt Gwen since Case told her it'd kill his grandparents to hear the crap she'd been pulling. Instead, she let Claire show off all the things she'd learned.

Later, as Gabbie sat by Papa Teddy, wrangling the kids during Case's graduation, she soon learned she was just as accepted by Nana and Papa as she had been by the Thomases. All they wanted was for their grandchildren to be loved and protected, and that Gabbie did with all her heart.

Chapter Fourteen

"The most exciting phrase to hear in science, the one that heralds new discoveries, is not "Eureka!" ("I found it!") but rather "hmm...that's funny..."

—*Isaac Asimov*

To be woken up by a very warm hand can sometimes be delightful, but when the hand is small and attached to a toddler, it doesn't have the same connotations. In fact, it's a warning that a warm hand from a lover is far from your future.

"Daddy Ace," Charlie said as he shook Case's bare forearm that was wrapped around Gabbie's soft body. "Daddy Ace."

"What's up, little man?" Case's groggy voice asked.

"Daddy, I coughed."

Case did have to say Gabbie had improved the twin's language skills, though he didn't see any reason to get up for a throat tickle.

"Are you done coughing?" he asked, trying to lift his heavy lids to see Charlie had climbed into bed and was leaning on Gabbie's hip.

Gabbie mumbled something as she snuggled tighter to Case's bare chest.

"I coughed all ober mys bed."

Either Case was still asleep or he was missing something important.

"Baby," he said, shaking Gabbie's shoulder. She responded by rolling over in his arms and latching on to his bicep. "Baby," he tried again. "I need a toddler translator. How do you cough all over your bed?"

"Huh? What are you talking about?" she shifted and started to sit up.

"I coughdided mama," Charlie said with sad eyes. "All obers mys bed."

"Coughed?" Gabbie asked waking up more. She looked at Case who shrugged his shoulders. "You're so helpful," Gabbie said stretching and adjusting her lilac cami so it was covering her stomach.

"I thinks I gonna cough again," Charlie said.

Gabbie woke up as if she had been hit with a thousand volts and reacted with lightning speed, grabbing the trash bin by Case's bed.

"I know that look," she said as Charlie threw up in the basket. "Case, he's a little warm."

"Icky," Charlie cried with tears streaming down his cheeks.

"I know little man. Let's get you cleaned up."

Gabbie carried Charlie down to the bathroom and Case heard the water running. Utter fear shot through him, thinking about what the bed must look like. But his son just came to him for help. So, pushing up off the bed, Case walked down the hall to see Gabbie with Case 'coughing' again into the toilet.

"You might want to check on Claire."

"I was going to strip his bed," Case said as he braced against the doorjamb.

"I've never loved you more than at this moment," Gabbie said.

"Why?"

"Because we're partners, and you're not shying away from the bad parts of the world."

"Take care of your kid, lady," Case said and the smile on Gabbie's face made it all worth it.

Charlie coughed on more than the bed. The bed had vomit on the pillow and sheets, but the table with his basketball lamp on it had a new coat to it. Then there was the carpet with spots everywhere. The first thing that came to Case's mind was how scary it was for Charlie to have this happen and be alone.

Case had checked on Claire, who was dead to the world around her. A light snore came from her side of the room as Case cleaned up and started the wash. Gabbie stopped in, picked up some fresh pajamas for Charlie, and also checked on Claire.

"She's got a fever too," Case said.

"I don't feel it," Gabbie said feeling Claire's forehead.

"Check her feet."

"What?"

"There are a few things I know. When I was little I got my fevers in my paws. At least that's what my mother always said. Her feet are on fire."

"We should wake her up to give her some Tylenol."

"Yeah. I was waiting on you for that. You mind if we all sleep together tonight?"

"Charlie's already in our bed."

"Our bed. That's the first time you didn't call it my bed."

"That okay?" Gabbie asked, scooping Claire into her arms.

"It's overdue. So is the little box in my nightstand," Case said and Gabbie winced. Case started to guide them down the hallway to his room.

"What little box?"

Case took Claire from Gabbie and placed her next to Charlie with Lucy curled up on his stomach. The picture before Case was missing one thing. A mixed race baby with soft curls being held in Gabbie's arms. Only that could make his family complete.

Getting down on one knee he reached into his nightstand for the black velvet box he'd been hiding from Gabbie for the past two weeks.

Her hands covered her mouth and he pulled down her left hand.

"I think we've seen the better and worse. We've now seen the sickness and health. If you promise me that you're not settling for me," Case said and Gabbie laughed.

Flipping the box open with one hand, Case took the plunge. Inside the box was a platinum band with a simple one-carat princess cut diamond. Along the band were three diamonds on each side. The jeweler had showed Case a dozen designs for the attached wedding band for Gabbie to pick out later. Tears were pooling in Gabbie's sparkling gray eyes.

"I want to make it official—you and me. I don't want to play house. I want this to be our house—with our kids—and you as my wife."

* * * *

"You wanna take the kids to Como?" Gabbie asked Case over breakfast the next morning. "Whatever they had is gone."

"Are you sure?"

He wasn't about to take two sick kids to Como Park. That place was hard on kids on a good day. With a zoo, the gardens in the conservatory, all the playgrounds, rides and games, you could wear out anyone in a few hours, especially a little kid if you weren't careful.

"Looks that way. Then maybe we could have a barb-b-que tonight," Gabbie said sheepishly as she put her breakfast dishes into the sink.

"What was that? Why are you being passive?"

"I could invite my dad and the girls. You could invite a few of your friends," Gabbie said as she rinsed the dishes and put them into the dishwasher.

"You're bursting at the seams aren't you?"

Gabbie turned around pink flushed cheeks and a smile that could put any supermodel to shame.

"Most of my friends aren't back from school yet, but I'm sure we could get some people together tomorrow."

"Tomorrow?"

"Barb-b-que is an all day adventure."

"Is it now?"

"Ribs, beans, burgers, hotdogs…"

"We'd have to go shopping again," Gabbie beamed and Case couldn't help feeling pride in how much she enjoyed their last adventure.

"After the park. Are the rides open yet?"

"I think so. We got a flyer the other day."

"Alright. Pack the monsters up and we'll head out."

The rides at Como were open for a sneak peek weekend. That meant the park was packed. Not what Case wanted, but a Saturday with his family would be fun. They spent the first half of the day walking through the zoo section of the park looking at the emperor monkeys, polar bears and lions. They took pictures of the kids on the bronze statues of the gorillas and giraffe.

Case remembered how much he loved coming to the zoo when he was younger. When they were in the penguin habitat, he saw the old machine that made waxy plastic figures of the animals. Gabbie had

126

Claire and Charlie out of the stroller. They were plastered against the glass watching the penguins playing in the water. He looked back to the machine and could see his mother standing there.

She was younger, her hair pulled back into a ponytail. She wore a white T-shirt tucked into her blue jean shorts. There was a stain from where he'd dropped his bomb pop. Case wished what he was seeing was more than a memory, but he knew better. He walked to the machine and dropped six quarters in. The familiar smell of melting plastic brought his father to the other side of the machine. His gut clenched, seeing his parents again. With a plunk, the light blue polar bear dropped into the bin and he retrieved it.

Case then realized he should have let the twins watch the toy being made. That's what his grandmother had let him do when he was little.

"Are you okay?" Gabbie asked as she stroked his back between his shoulder blades.

"Am I going to be able to give them what my parents gave me?" he asked as his hand burned slightly against the warm plastic figure.

"Your parents bought you those?"

"Grandma... My parents lectured me on how it was a waste of money because I always lost them before I even got out of the park. They used to bring me here a lot. I know every plant in the conservatory. I put in names for the monkeys when they were born."

"Did they use them?"

"I don't think so. Gabbie, I had a great childhood."

"Yeah, why don't you think you can give Claire and Charlie the same thing?"

Case wiped a tear from his cheek and braced himself against the machine. Gabbie wrapped her arms around his chest and held herself against his back.

"Case. I'm here for you. I'll always be here for you."

Case turned around and held her tight to his body. He clutched her as if his life depended on it. Burying his nose in her hair, he pulled in the sweet, soft smell of her shampoo and felt stronger. After a minute, she pulled back and brought her lips to his. This wasn't the passion they seemed to find around each other. Instead, it was just a gentle peck that confirmed everything he needed at that moment.

"We can do it."

"That's what I like to hear. How about we go have some lunch?"

"Gabbie, I'm sorry that..."

"Shh," she said as she placed a finger over his lips. "I think every first after you've lost someone is going to be a challenge. Your parents can see the amazing job you're doing. They are smiling down with the same pride they had when they were alive."

"I love you, Gabbie, you know that right?"

"I got that impression a couple of times?"

By lunch time, the kids were starting to show signs of fading and Case didn't want to admit he was a little happy about that. Gabbie had packed a picnic lunch for everyone so they went out to the conservatory lawn to eat.

Gabbie relaxed in between Case's legs and the kids sat eating their peanut butter and grape jelly sandwiches that Gabbie had cut into fourths. The bugs weren't heavy yet since it was early May. Instead, the sun beamed down on their little piece of heaven as they sat next to the reflecting pond that surrounded the large glass green house that served as the conservatory. Across from them the Cafesjian Carousel played a song from the turn of the century.

"We have to take them to the carousel, even if we don't go to Como Town," Case said.

"You know I've never ridden on that carousel."

"It'll be the first time since I was about ten so we'll have to get side-by-side horses for the kids."

"They're getting a second wind," Gabbie said as Claire and Charlie got up and started to chase each other around Gabbie and Case.

Case reached out and caught Claire. He flipped her upside down as she squealed and her skirt covered her eyes.

"Daddy..."

"Momma, have you seen Claire?" Case asked Gabbie.

"No," Gabbie said as she caught Charlie and squeezed him tight. "Have you seen Claire, Charlie?"

"Mama Care upside."

"She's upside?" Gabbie said as she turned so her head was on the blanket looking in the clouds. "She's not upside... I don't see her."

"Mama, Daddy gots her."

"Are you sure?"

"Mama," Charlie said with all seriousness as he placed two chubby hands on Gabbie's cheeks. "She's upside on Daddy."

"Well so she is." Gabbie smiled at Case who flipped Claire back into his lap. "Should we clean up so we can go on rides?"

Charlie was the first to pick up the Tupperware containers that were strewn all over the blanket. Gabbie grabbed the trash and walked it to a bin as Case started to reload the cooler. Claire bunched up the blanket and stuffed it into the basket under the stroller.

Case intertwined his fingers with Gabbie's as they pushed the double stroller up the hill toward the carousel. Gabbie leaned against Case's arm and he couldn't keep the smile from crossing his lips. The last person he wanted to be was his father when he was younger and here he was with the love of his life, walking his kids in Como Park and he couldn't be happier.

The Cafesjian Carousel had at least sixty hand carved horses, cats, and other animals all done in the style of the early nineteen hundreds. If they didn't have the kids, Case would have talked Gabbie into snuggling with him in one of the stationary sleds. The center had mirrors that caught the small lights and the singing of the ragtime music. They buckled each twin to a horse and stood next to each other, snagging kisses when the kids were focused on where they were going instead of their parents.

After the carousel, they headed to the bigger amusement park. Como Town had been little more than cheap carnival rides when Case had been a kid, but it had been updated a few years ago so the mini rollercoaster was safe enough now that Case was comfortable enough to take the kids on it.

"How about I go grab some mini-donuts while you take the kids on the coaster?"

"You scared?" Case laughed as he looked at the rollercoaster that only went up and down in a circle.

"I smelled them. I can't not have 'em."

Pulling Gabbie close, Case inhaled the sweet smell of her hair and kissed her neck softly.

"I understand the draw," he growled against her neck and felt her shiver in his arms.

By the time Case got through the line, Gabbie was back standing on the other side of the railing eating mini-donuts from the small white paper bag with red writing on it. She smiled as she licked some sugar that had gotten stuck on her top lip. The blush across her cheeks let him know she meant for him to see her and he had to shift in the coaster's car to make his erection settle back down.

They went around once with Gabbie waving at them, then on the second pass he saw her talking to a taller guy with shaggy blond hair. He was wearing the same shirt as all the rest of the Como Park employees. Gabbie rolled the top of the donut bag down and tucked it away as if in shame as the guy pointed back and forth at it and her ass.

The body language coming off Gabbie had Case ready to jump out of the car and rush to her. Three more passes and Gabbie's hand was clutching the stroller's dark blue padded handle for support. Her eyes cut to the stroller when the guy pointed to it and she pulled it closer.

"Daddy…" Claire squealed because he hadn't raised his arms when then went down the small slope.

"Sorry baby," Case said. His eyes stayed locked on Gabbie.

The guy raised his hand toward Gabbie's cheek and Case stood up only to have the safety bar cut into his thigh as he crashed back to the seat. Pain shot through his legs and he knew he bruised himself, but all he wanted to do was get off the damn ride. Gabbie stepped back and finally lifted her head to glare at the guy. Case smiled at that. He wasn't sure if it was the fact that Gabbie had dropped her eyes like she was some weakling or that a guy was talking to her that pissed him off more. All he knew was his stomach was doing summersaults, and it had nothing to do with the ride.

The second the ride stopped he unlatched the safety bar and snatched Claire and Charlie, who were a little discombobulated, into his arms as he rushed through the exit gate.

"So are you a nanny now?" the guy asked as Case approached.

"No."

"But you're still a baby sitter?"

"She's a teacher," Case said, catching their attention.

Gabbie looked up at him and he could see relief wash over her face. Case scanned the guy and found a nametag; Kirk. He should have known.

"Kirk, this is Case Thomas—"

"Her fiancée," Case interjected.

"I was getting there," Gabbie said and took Charlie.

"Not fast enough."

"That explains why you're still eating like the pig you were in high school."

"Pig?" Case snapped.

"Hey, I know black guys like 'em thick and all…"

"She's a frickin' twig."

"Off a redwood maybe," he said as he scanned Gabbie's hips.

Case could feel his heart start to race. Shit talkers in games he could handle. Tell him he's nothing. Tell him he couldn't score in a brothel. Tell him they were surprised his ass could move with all the splinters from the bench in it. Block his shot, foul him, get up in his face…he stayed in control. Make his woman look down in shame and question her amazing body…*you will pay.*

"I heard you didn't even know what to do with a woman. Or do you prefer the company of little boys? Women have curves," Case informed him.

"So does a ball, but I don't want to fuck it. No grown woman babysits for a living."

"She's a teacher."

"She wipes little kid's asses. That's a baby sitter."

"I heard she got a lot of hands-on experience her senior year with that skill, and watch your language around our kids," Case growled. "She's a teacher who started her own school. What are you, a cotton candy guy?"

"Your kids? I hadn't heard of you poppin' out any puppies. That explains those hips."

"Puppies," Case said as he passed Claire to Gabbie. "I understand if you had kids they'd be some crossed section between a lizard and a mammal, but what does or doesn't pop out of Gabbie is none of your damn business."

"They're not yours are they?" Kirk said, looking around Case and pissing him off more.

This guy was acting as if Case was some kind of punk that would take crap off him. Gabbie was right. This guy thought his shit didn't stink. He was about to learn a lesson and it wasn't going to be from a teacher this time.

"I should have known the only guy you could get was someone desperate for a maid."

"Gabbie, leave," Case ordered. "Walk away now. Kirk and I have something's to get clear."

"No, we don't. Have fun being a doormat Gabbie, I know how much a whore like you enjoys being laid out and stepped on."

Case's rage was only tempered by the fact he wasn't about to go off in front of his kids. It was bad enough they saw Gabbie snap out last week. To have him do the same...*awe fuck it.*

His fist stayed clenched as he stepped toward Kirk. Case tried to stare him down, but the weak ass wouldn't look him in the eyes. Case had him.

"Don't ever talk to her again. You hear me. You punk-assed-pussy. Sayin' all she is, is an ass wiping baby sitter. She's a teacher, who owns and manages her own business. What the hell are you?"

"I work for the city," he sneered and Case laughed.

"In rides, games, or fast food?"

"Fuck you."

"I told you to watch your language around my kids."

"What the hell are you going to do about it?"

Kirk stepped into Case's personal space. The break in the air around Case sent a tingle up his spine. He knew the sensation and wasn't sure how much longer he could maintain control.

"That's what I thought, Bitch."

"Bitch? You've got to be kidding me. Don't get me twisted with you. I'm bigger than you'll ever be, because I have her supporting me."

"Oh, you're payin' his way. That makes sense."

"I work in R and D at *3M*...You know *3M* right? When you clean up kids' puke you probably use our gloves."

"So she just watches the kids your baby momma didn't even want."

It was at that point Case would like to say he blacked out. He'd like to say he lost control and couldn't remember what happened. But as his knuckles made contact with the left side of Kirk's face he felt every sweet sting as the guy's cheek bone crackled against his fist. Blood rushed through his body as he took in every sound that gurgled out of the guy's mouth. And when he fell back into the gate, then bounced to the ground, the satisfaction Case felt as if he heard the air rush out of his lungs with a thump brought him back to the state finals his junior year— a positive win.

Smiling, he turned to Gabbie who was staring at him with her mouth agape.

"Daddy naughy likes mama," Claire said.

"No, Claire," Gabbie said as she stepped into Case's arms. "Daddy's mama's hero."

Chapter Fifteen

*"You know you're in love when you can't fall asleep because your
reality is finally better than your dreams."*
—Dr. Seuss

The next morning, Gabbie still had no idea how they all got out of
the park unscathed. She was sure Case was going to be hauled off to jail
or at least be confronted by other employees. Instead, it seemed Kirk had
more enemies than friends at work. Little did she know how turned on
she'd become from having a man defend her honor. *Oh sure,* she
thought, *you see the idea in movies, but to actually have a man stick up
for you...*it had a very positive effect on her. She had trapped Case
against the car after the kids were buckled in. He'd acted like it had been
nothing when she practically took him by force right out in the open.

"You know I could always look into becoming a boxer," Case
whispered against her neck as the warm morning sun broke through his
eastern facing window.

"It wasn't the fight."

"Wasn't it?" Case practically cooed at her.

"Nope. It was the reason for the fight."

"You have anyone else that's an asshole when it comes to you?"

"Not that I can recall."

"Would you please find some?"

"I'll see what I can do."

Outside the door, they heard a few thumps and giggles.

"You think they'll give us a half hour?" Case teased as his nose brushed against Gabbie's neck causing her to shiver in his arms. The door blew open as Claire and Charlie rushed the bed, breaking the cool calm of their morning.

"My monsters," Case growled as he caught both of them in his arms.

Gabbie loved to see the way his biceps flexed as he held the twins tight and swirled them in the bed. She jumped out of the bed to avoid the wrestling match that had Charlie and Claire riding on Case's back. Gabbie leaned against the desk and took in the moment. She smiled, thinking this was the way she'd get to wake up on the weekends for the rest of her life.

Her finger twirled the ring that fit perfectly on her left ring finger. Two months. Oh. My. God. The reality of her situation hit her gut first causing a cramp, then to her chest as she tried to catch her breath. Finally, her head spun and she had to brace her hands on either side of the desk.

She'd never even introduced Case to her dad. *He lives five minutes away.* Did she tell him that she'd moved in? She had to have? Hadn't she? It's okay. She'd just be introducing her father to her fiancée.

Engaged? She had pledged herself to Case for life. Or she'd agreed to pledge herself. How could she explain this to her friends and family that she'd invited over today? What was she thinking? She'd gone from single to married with two kids in…

"Mama," Charlie said with a tone that stopped the tickle fest that had started when Case had flipped the kids off his back.

Charlie jumped off the bed and hugged her legs, looking up with his deep mahogany eyes. Every worry seemed to disappear when she looked into a Thomas man's eyes, even if he was only two. Whether it was Case saying she was who he wanted as his wife, or Charlie calling her his mother, the sincerity and love behind those eyes told her she'd made the right decision.

"Are you okay, Baby?"

Gabbie leaned down and scooped Charlie into her arms. His chubby arms wrapped around her neck and squeezed.

"Yes, we need to get ready for the party."

"Are you sure?" Case said as he came to Gabbie and pushed back her hair so he could see her eyes. "You look a little pale."

"Something about the Thomas pile made me smile."

"It wasn't a full pile," Case said, pulling Gabbie and Charlie back on the bed. Claire jumped on top. "We needed our foundation."

With Gabbie on the bottom of the Thomas pile she felt crushed and loved as Case and the kids took it upon themselves to tickle, hug, and kiss her until she'd completely lost control—laughing, smiling and she knew was loved. Thinking back, the challenges they had faced seemed small in comparison to the joy Gabbie felt. Sadly, a storm was forming in the distance, threatening to tear the Thomas family apart and seeking shelter was not an option. They would have to band together or risk being scattered to the wind.

Case had rubbed down the ribs and the kitchen smelled amazing. Gabbie looked out the back window over the sink in the kitchen to see Case getting the coals ready. Claire and Charlie were playing on the small wood swing set in the backyard. Gabbie was dicing celery for the cold shrimp salad.

The twins rushed in and Gabbie gave them a small snack before putting them down for a nap so they'd last through the party. Afterward, Case found her looking lost at the island in the kitchen.

"Are you sure you're okay?" Case asked as he leaned across the island and held her hands in his. Case let his thumbs gently stroke the back of her hands.

"The last time I talked to my dad we weren't together."

"And…"

"That was like two months ago."

"You aren't close?"

"We are, but he understands I get distracted between work and school. He's not an obtrusive man. He takes me when I'm available."

"What's the issue, Gabbie?"

"I'm going to be telling him that I gave up my apartment, moved in with a guy and I'm going to marry him after two months."

"That sounds bad," Case said. "I'd kill Claire if she did something like that."

"See…"

"But I'm not your dad, am I?" Case prodded, making Gabbie look up at him.

"No."

"And it's not like we ran off to Vegas."

"Yeah."

"And it's not like we don't love each other."

"That is a plus."

"And I'm handsome, gainfully employed and gave you two kids without the pain of labor."

"You keep bringing that up."

"My mom liked to use how long her labor was with me as reason that I owed her."

"Smart woman. But have you really done that? What's up with the custody battle?"

"I will get custody," Case said matter-of-factly. "And after we're married, maybe we'll have some the old fashion way."

"I don't know. You keep scaring me with this whole labor thing…"

"Drugs are better now."

"You want more kids?"

"You don't?"

"I would like to have at least one," Gabbie smiled.

"Just one?"

"How many do you want?"

"I think I just want to make them."

"It is fun."

"Don't worry about your dad, okay? Dads love me."

"Just don't tell him we're practicing making babies."

"Hell no. I want to live…at least until my wedding night."

At three, Gabbie woke the twins up from a nap. Most of the food was ready and everyone would be arriving by four. Gabbie looked at Charlie and Claire and the thought of her dad came back to her. Would he accept them as his grandchildren? Maybe she should have called and warned him that she was dating a black guy. Maybe she should have told him she was living with a guy in general. Their little talk a few months ago couldn't have foreshadowed where she was now.

"Mama," Claire whined when Gabbie redid her hair for the third time. She just wanted to have her dad see them as perfect as she did.

"I'm sorry, Claire, mama's just a little nervous."

"Why?"

"Because mama thinks you and Charlie are the most wonderful kids in the whole world and you are going to meet mama's daddy and I want him to think the same thing."

"I 'fused mama," Claire replied. "Hows come you gots a daddy?"

"Why shouldn't I have a daddy?"

"Daddy no gots a daddy."

"Daddy had a wonderful daddy and you have Papa Teddy right?"

"Is yous daddy a papa?" Charlie asked.

"Kinda. Mommy has to talk to him about that first."

This day was becoming more and more complicated by the minute. How was she going to deal with melding this family? Gabbie finally saw why her dad stayed single.

As the guests arrived, Gabbie stayed guarded. Her left hand wasn't hidden, but it wasn't going to be flaunted. People brought salads and drinks that she placed in the kitchen. Case finally finished the ribs and was cutting them apart when the doorbell rang. It had to be her dad.

"Okay," Gabbie said as she and Case walked to the door. "Don't be nervous. My dad is going to love you."

"Why would I be nervous?"

Gabbie opened the door to see her dad standing next to a woman who appeared to be in her forties. She had sandy brown hair pushed back with a set of black sunglasses. She appeared as uncomfortable as Gabbie.

"Hi, Dad," Gabbie said, as she hugged him. "Um…Dad, this is Case."

"Nice to meet you in person," her dad said as he shook Case's hand. He then leaned in close. "About that thing we discussed…"

"We'll talk more later."

"What thing?" Gabbie asked.

"Don't worry," Case replied and kissed Gabbie's cheek. "You must be Linda?"

Case escorted her father and Linda to the backyard. Gabbie called for Claire and Charlie to come over.

"Dad, this is Claire and Charlie, Case's…kids."

"Wees most wonderful righ?" Claire asked plainly and Gabbie blushed.

"You seem that way," her dad said as squatted down to look the kids in the eye.

"So you papa?" Charlie asked and Gabbie curled into Case's chest unable to breathe from embarrassment. She should have known the kids wouldn't hold back.

"I'm not sure, Case?"

"No time like the present," Case said as he raised his voice. "Everyone, can we have your attention?"

"What are you doing?" Gabbie murmured as she looked up at Case who just winked and held her tighter.

"This isn't just a barb-b-que. A few days ago, Gabbie agreed to marry me."

Oh crap, Gabbie thought. *It's out there now.* With her face on fire, Gabbie turned around, holding her hand up. She looked around the yard to see a mixture of shocked and smiling faces.

The world seemed to slow down. Or maybe it was just in her head that no one moved. Then came the squeal from Linda, which started a chain reaction with Mandy, Mary Beth and Sarah rushing her with congratulations. Case's friends Paul, Traun and Tyreek all came over and shook his hand too.

Claire pulled on Gabbie's shirt to get her attention.

"Mama…mama…mama…"

"Yes, baby."

"Is he papa?"

Gabbie looked over at her father with tears pooled in his eyes as he came over and hugged her.

"I was so happy when Case called me to ask for your hand," her dad gushed.

Gabbie turned toward Case, who smiled.

"Yes, Claire, he's your papa Maury," Case said as he kissed the back of Gabbie's neck. "I love you, baby. Don't be mad I called your dad."

"Hungry mama," Charlie said and that started the parade to the buffet.

During dinner, the subject of the summer softball league came up. Gabbie's dad was first to volunteer to add Charlie and Claire to his babysitting duties during the day. For the last three years, Luke had been his softball buddy in the stands. It's not like the league had practices.

"Are you going to join?" Mandy asked Case as she leaned against the edge of the patio table.

"Um…"

"Don't feel any pressure. You can hang with dad in the stands," Gabbie said. "But it is a co-ed team."

"I heard you could really handle a bat," Mandy growled and Gabbie shoved her shoulder so she fell on the ground.

"Oh, Mandy, has that inner ear problem not cleared up yet?" Gabbie teased as the whole table erupted with laughter.

Case leaned into Gabbie and kissed her neck then extended his hand to pull Mandy up off the grass.

"Yous falls down, Ms. Mand," Claire giggled with a carrot in her hand.

"Yes." Mandy grumbled and dusted off her shorts. "I'm silly, huh?"

Luke and Charlie were laughing at their crazy teacher who was now laughing at herself. *Hopefully she'll remember next time to keep her mouth shut*, Gabbie thought.

* * * *

Everyone helped out cleaning up in the kitchen. Case nudged Gabbie with his hip as they rinsed the dishes together before they put them in the dishwasher.

"You been talkin' about my bat?"

"No," Gabbie said aghast. "I swear."

"Must be that smile that's permanently glued to her face," Sarah said as she sealed up the last of the shrimp salad in containers.

"It has been around a lot lately," Case beamed with pride.

"I'm gonna go save my dad from the kids," Gabbie said, embarrassed, as she rushed out of the kitchen.

Case eyed Sarah, who suddenly seemed nervous and retreated also. Mary Beth walked into the kitchen then stepped back when she realized everyone had gone to the backyard.

"Hello," she said with unease.

"Mary Beth," Case began as he rested his back against the counter.

"Could I ask you something?"

"I suppose."

"What did Kirk do to her? Was it just normal…I don't know…we ran into him yesterday…"

"Kirk? You ran into to Kirk? Sorry to hear a semi hasn't done that yet."

Okay, it's obvious the hatred for the guy seemed to come from those who know him, Case mused. *But there has to be more to it than he was a jackass.*

"What's the story?"

"I'm not surprised Gabbie hasn't told you, but I don't know the full depth of their relationship, if you could call it that."

"I thought you girls shared everything."

"We have our roles. I'm the mom when people have the flu, Sarah's the one you want to go to the bar with—"

"Sarah?"

"Sarah can drink you under the table and have you dancing on it at the same time. She's fun as hell."

"I thought that was Mandy's job."

"Mandy…Mandy's the friend you want when someone's pissed you off beyond reason. She's not afraid of hurting a guy or doing major damage to property."

"That's not shocking. So what's Gabbie's role?"

"Gabbie's…Gabbie's…well she keeps us together—I guess the other mom of our group. She makes plans that I usually make sure work, like Growing Strong. Gabbie found the place. I kept it afloat as we transitioned with the original owner over the first year. If you want to know what happened between Gabbie and Kirk, I'd say ask Mandy, because Gabbie'll never tell."

"Maybe I shouldn't go behind her back."

"On this you should. You'll avoid minefields."

"That bad?"

"I'm surprised she let you touch her. Guys used to hit on her and she'd scare them away with a look. If they tried to touch her…she'd deck 'em."

Case couldn't believe his amiable Gabbie could possibly be that cold to men. Now Case needed to find out what Kirk did to her. As he looked out into the backyard, he saw Mandy chatting up Paul and Tyreek in the Adirondack chairs under the maple tree. *No time like the present.*

"Guys, I need to talk to my girl Mandy here for a second. Could you give us some space?"

"Um… They're single, you're not. Move on, Case."

"It's about Gabbie. Please, Amanda Sue," Case said as Mandy glared at him.

"Yeah, sure man," Paul complied. "I needed something to drink anyway. You want anything, Mandy?"

"Just water. That'll give Case here three minutes," Mandy cooed as she let her fingers stroke Paul's bicep.

Case should have known Mandy would have glommed on to his friends. Tyreek didn't move. Instead, he shifted in his seat and leaned in closer to Mandy.

"Later," Mandy teased when Tyreek placed his hand on her knee. "The old guy wants to talk about *my girl*."

Alone, Case sat down and positioned himself like they were just chatting about the weather.

"What?" Mandy snipped.

"I was told you were the one who knew about Kirk."

"Kirk the jerk."

"That'd be the one."

"Small dick, no personality, and an inferiority complex that rivaled Napoleon. Anything else?"

"What happened between him and Gabbie?"

"If she didn't tell, why should I?"

"Because he can turn her into a shy coward that can't look a man in the eye," Case said as he turned to look at Mandy. "And *my girl* doesn't play bitch to anyone."

Mandy seemed to respect Case's inflection. Even though she looked like she hadn't decided if she should tell him or not, Case knew one thing, Mandy respected Gabbie and knew how strong she was.

"It took her a long time to come back to being that girl after Kirk." Mandy sighed and leaned back in her chair.

"Why?"

"You know how dumb people will try to make smart people feel stupid?"

Case understood the concept, but never saw the draw himself.

"Kirk was perfect at first. Gabbie had talked to guys, but she doesn't see them as sexual objects." Case wanted to disagree with Mandy on that point. "I don't mean everyone, obviously. You've had her panties in a regular Gooseberry Falls since she laid eyes on you, but you know how most guys at least have a chance with a girl. Not with Gabbie. Most guys are seen as unisex. Much like girls sadly," Mandy said as she inspected her nails.

"Are you in love with her?" Case asked.

"I'd kill for her."

"Is that a warning?"

"One I forgot to give Kirk," Mandy said as she stretched with a devilish grin.

"You didn't answer my question."

"Why do you care?" Mandy asked as her head rolled from one shoulder then another.

"Because we're in love with the same woman."

"But I'm not competition."

"For her time, you are."

"I've noticed that I've gotten way less than I deserve lately."

"You think I'm monopolizing her."

"The only time Gabbie was with a guy he domineered over her. There are some guys...you seem to be one of them, that Gabbie would give the world to. Kirk was one of them. He never acknowledged her in public, but she didn't see that as a negative."

Case settled in, ready to hear the tale from the girl's side of the story. All the girls hated Kirk. At first they were happy when Gabbie would call them to tell how Kirk had done this or that, but soon they realized it was only in the evening. In school he'd still flirt with other girls, even going as far as to pick them up and carry them around school while they all giggled, which Case found out was a big no-no. Everyone had thought that Kirk was a player that didn't settle down.

To say he cheated on Gabbie would be an understatement. It was the way that he did it. He manipulated her so she felt she couldn't go on without him. She isolated herself from the girls because he made her be the swim team's manager. It kept her away from the weightlifting and training the girls had done the past few seasons. Gabbie barely saw them in between classes.

She was no longer the girl she had been. Her eyes seemed vacant and she always had dark circles. She lost at least fifteen pounds in a few months.

"It was freezing out when she stood on my stoop," Mandy said with remorseful eyes. "He finally had gone too far. She'd been walking for hours in February of all months. They had a meet in South St. Paul and afterward Kirk convinced her to go to his friend's house."

Mandy's eyes turned to rage as she looked at Case and he could tell by her tone the black eye he'd given Kirk yesterday wasn't enough.

"He tried to force her to go down on his friend while he watched. He told her that it would turn him on. Since she wasn't a sexy girl this would be the only way he could get it up. It's not like they hadn't had sex before then, if you can call it that. Somehow he'd convinced her if she loved him the way he loved her, she'd do it. He just wanted to humiliate her and call her a whore when she was done."

"That doesn't even sound like Gabbie."

"I know. The next day the rumors started about how she 'creamed her jeans' the second she saw him."

"Who says creamed her jeans?"

"Someone who ended up with three quarts of half and half in his gas tank when temps hit the upper nineties," Mandy beamed with pride. "He made it out like the whole relationship had been in her head—that she was some simple puppy that'd been following him around for months, not that he'd been sending her emails and calling her every night until two in the morning. The worst part is he made it so she didn't trust herself. Here she'd deluded herself for a guy that made her think the reason she couldn't come was her fault. Somehow, he made her feel like a frigid prude and slut in the same condescending comment."

"Why?"

"He's miserable. She can make anyone happy when she decides to love them. She gives herself fully. Please don't abuse that."

"I won't. I promise."

"I hope so. At least one good thing came of her being with Kirk."

"And that would be?"

"We won sectionals. By the way, how were the batting cages when you went there to get her?"

"Eye opening. You know you're always welcome at our house," Case said, although part of him didn't want to have an open-door policy.

"That's why you're still alive."

"Tell me one thing. If you love her so much, why have you put so much effort into making her think she's not as attractive as she is?" Case asked as he smiled at Gabbie across the lawn.

The sun was trickling through the leaves of the neighbor's poplar tree, leaving little starbursts on her cheeks. Her dark hair was no longer tight to her head; a few loose strands had fallen on either side of her now pinked cheeks, but it was her smile that had both Case and Mandy warming in their chests. Gabbie's teeth glistened between her perfect rose lips and her eyes danced as she listened lovingly to her father recanting a story. In her arms, Claire snuggled into the nook below her shoulder and curled her fingers around Gabbie's as she deftly twisted the engagement ring to catch the light. Neither Case nor Mandy knew what she was hearing, but they both knew that Gabbie verged on euphoria, surrounded by her family and friends.

"Because when I told her how beautiful she was, she fell for Kirk, not me."

Chapter Sixteen

"I may not have gone where I intended to go, but I think I have ended up where I needed to be."

—*Douglas Adams*

Gabbie spun her engagement ring on her finger. It'd been three long months since Case's Aunt Gwen had barged into the daycare center, and now Gabbie sat behind Case in the courthouse for Washington County, dressed in her first business suit. It was navy blue with pinstripes and made her feel like she was fifty years old. Sure Case told her he loved that it hugged her curves and made her look like a sexy business woman, but he could make anything she wore feel sexy from the way his deep voice described the curve of her hips or the way her hair would flow down her back. It didn't matter, Case found it attractive.

Case's suit on the other hand did make him look sexy as hell. She looked at him with his dreads tied back, his dark glasses framing his intelligent eyes, and his father's watch on his wrist. Case was used to the finer things. His suit was custom made at Christmas in anticipation of his graduation. The watch came from an exclusive jeweler in the west metro, but his parents had worked for every penny and Case didn't let that life lesson pass him by.

The twins' trust fund had gone virtually untouched since Case's first few paychecks cleared. Together they were assuming all financial responsibility.

"Are we ready to proceed?" the judge asked.

"My claimant hasn't arrived yet," Gwen's attorney said, with his best apologetic voice.

"Your claimant has delayed these proceedings more times than I think my patience can allow," the judge advised. "Outside of tormenting this young man and dragging out an adoption that should have flown through this court months ago, what is your claimant's stand concerning the minor children involved?"

"She feels that she was left out of the whole process in determining a proper guardian for the minor children involved."

Gabbie could see the vein on the side of Case's head start to bulge out and his right fist clench. He hated when Claire and Charlie were referred to as the minor children as if they were chattel.

"What right in determining this guardianship does she assert? I have the DNA evidence forwarded by the lab stating although there are familial markers she is not the genetic mother. The children are in fact genetic matches for the primary claimant in this filing, their brother Case Thomas, which, without unearthing the mother in question, proves beyond a shadow of a doubt your claimant is not the mother of the minor children involved."

Case turned and looked at Gabbie. She nodded, understanding this meant Case should have no problem getting the kids.

The doors swung open as Gwen traipsed in as if she was early instead of almost a half hour late. She and her husband took their seats next to their attorney, who nodded to the judge as he relayed the DNA evidence to her.

Gwen's face became ashen as if she had been hit by a truck as her husband sat with a scowl across his face. Gabbie saw Gwen trying to placate her husband.

"In fact," the judge continued, even more irritated then before, "the extra cost incurred not only by this court and the primary claimant in attorney's fees should be paid by yours. But that is not for me to determine. My job is to place the minor children in the best environment for growth and development, which their parents clearly felt was with their eldest son and it was clearly stated in their will, updated upon their birth. The secondary claimant states the guardian in question is a college student and single parent, therefore unable to care for the minor children in question. So, Mr. Howard can you please present your case?"

"Case Thomas is gainfully employed by 3M in their R and D division. He was offered this position after successfully completing an internship during his senior year of college. He graduated Sum Cum Laude from the University of North Dakota in chemistry this last spring, all while taking care of the two minor children in question."

"By yourself?" the judge asked Case and Case looked at Gabbie as he stood to address the judge.

"No," he said. "My attorney wasn't aware I'm engaged to the woman my children call their mother now."

"Your children? Do you mean the minors in question?"

"Charlie and Claire call me dad," Case said, holding his voice firm.

"Why didn't you mention you had created a two-parent home?"

"Because it shouldn't matter. I started out as their brother, but I have taken on all the responsibilities of a father. I'm their dad. In my parents' will, they wanted me to raise them."

"What of this woman? You say they call her mother. What are her intentions? Are you planning on having women come in and out of their lives? The secondary claimant already has an established home in which the children can grow. You on the other hand have established that you have an unrelated woman caring for them without any legal commitment."

Case turned around and looked at Gabbie, who stood up and rested her hands on the divider between the court and the gallery. Case leaned into her ear and asked her what she wanted.

"I want to be their mom."

Case leaned down to Ron, who had taken his seat.

"Is it too late to amend the claim to add Gabbie Vaulst?" he asked.

"I could have put together the paperwork before we got here," Ron said, slightly disgusted. Then he shook his head. "Your Honor, I didn't know about this woman, but since they are soon to be wed, I indulge your already tried patience in closing this file today if we could add a Ms. Vaulst as joint claimant with Mr. Thomas."

"Objection, Your Honor," Gwen's attorney said while Gwen whispered in his ear. "How many claimants are there going to be for these two children? Should we just allow anyone to show up and lay claim to any child to establish a two family home?"

"Is that what your client is doing?" the judge asked.

"No, Your Honor. My client merely updated the situation. He is more than willing to take sole custody of the minors in question and then after his marriage, have his wife file separately."

"Excuse me." A woman stood up and came from the back of the courtroom.

Gabbie recognized her from somewhere. She had her brunette hair held back with a headband. Her green polo shirt was slightly untucked on her right side as she fumbled with a handful of files. The social worker.

"I'm Jessica Strong from Washington County DHS, I wrote the report on the Thomas household."

"And?" the judge asked.

"Ms...." she looked at Gabbie who stumbled over her thoughts.

"Vaulst."

"Right, Ms. Vaulst was noted as a secondary supervising adult and as day time caregiver in my report. I'm prepared to give my opinion on her fitness as an adoptive parent."

"Mr. Howard, do you have a paralegal that can amend the claim and have it here in thirty minutes?"

"Yes, Your Honor," Ron said, pulling out his phone and texting. He then passed the phone to Gabbie, who left the courtroom to answer questions in the hall.

When the paralegal came rushing through the doors of the courthouse, Gabbie felt her heart lurch. In that woman's hands were papers that would turn her into a mother. She'd be responsible for another human being. Scratch that, two human beings.

She thought back to her own mother and the few memories she had of her getting frustrated and snapping on her. No, she wasn't her mother, she thought as the woman finally cleared security.

"Gabrielle?" the woman asked, and for a split second Gabbie thought of turning away and leaving.

Then her dad walked through the door with Charlie and Claire.

"Mama," they both sang as they ran through the metal detector, thankfully not setting off any alarms.

Gabbie bent down and happily accepted their hugs. She watched as her dad emptied his pockets and walked through the metal detectors.

"What are you doing here?" Gabbie asked her dad as she stood up with a chubby little hand clutching each of hers.

"I heard my daughter was becoming a mother. Thought I'd come watch. It's not every day I get to become a grandfather."

Gwen and her legal team strode out of the courtroom past them and scowled as Gabbie pulled the children closer in fear that this woman would try some last-minute move.

"I would've been a great mother," Gwen snapped.

"You're still young," Gabbie said, proudly holding her children tight to her.

"So are you. You're not going to want them if you have your own children."

"Who dat mama?" Claire asked.

"That's your Auntie Gwen," Gabbie replied and Gwen winced. "They're my children," Gabbie stated plainly.

"You sure about that? He won custody. He doesn't need you anymore."

"He never needed me," Gabbie said with authority. "That's what you can't get. He wants me. Do you know the difference?"

"We have to get going, Ms. Vaulst," the paralegal said as she placed her hand on Gabbie's shoulder.

"They look at you and see a stranger. They'll never see themselves in you," Gwen hissed as Gabbie walked into the courtroom.

As they walked into the courtroom, Gabbie had never felt surer of anything in her life. Her dad took Charlie and Claire and sat them in the first row of the gallery as Gabbie walked into the courtroom and sat next to Case. Their fingers entwined as they listened to the judge.

"This is a county court of law, not your personal family court, Mr. Thomas, and Minnesota state law says you have to wait five days from obtaining a marriage license before you can legally get married," the judge said and Gabbie turned to Case, confused. "That being said, if Ms. Vaulst agrees, I'd like to postpone my decision for seven days. That way you can return and I'd be proud to perform the ceremony. After the testimony I've heard on behalf of your co-claimant, Ms. Vaulst, I'm impressed."

Case leaned into Gabbie's ear and whispered, "Had to try. When I ambush you, you never say no."

"Um…what did I miss?" Gabbie asked.

"Mr. Thomas requested I marry the two of you because it is not customary to allow a single woman to be a co-claimant on an adoption case. But your paperwork is in order. Would you like to adopt them as Gabrielle Vaulst or Gabrielle Thomas?"

"I…I…would there be any chance of someone else changing your decision of letting Case adopt if we waited seven days?"

"Anything is possible, but I'd say highly unlikely."

Gabbie looked into Case's mahogany eyes and smiled.

"Then, yes, I'd like to go for the twofer."

"We'll see you in seven days. You can obtain a license at the county clerk's office. I'd suggest sooner rather than later."

* * * *

"We're getting married in a week," Gabbie gasped as they left the courtroom.

"Too soon?" Case asked as he held her to him.

"Soon? Um…" Gabbie looked into his eyes and nibbled on her lower lip.

Case couldn't help but be nervous himself. In less than four months he'd become the father of two toddlers, found the love of his life and was now hoping to marry her. Case was worried until he heard the self-assured response from Gabbie.

"Not in the least."

"I promise you I will love and cherish you forever."

"Save those words for our wedding day."

"Well I guess I don't get to become a grandpa today," Gabbie's dad said as he Eskimo kissed Claire, who he held in his arms. "False labor drives me crazy."

If nothing else, Case loved Gabbie's dad and his simple ways. They only had about an hour to file for a marriage license, so they rushed to the city clerk and filled out the paperwork. Case somehow found a way to control an out-of-control situation and felt at ease for the first time in months.

"I guess we'll have to tell the girls," Case said as he spooned some ice cream into Gabbie's mouth that evening after the kids were asleep.

They were sitting on opposite ends of the couch with their legs a tangled mess in between.

"Yeah," she said, a little forlorn.

"What's wrong, Baby?"

"It's a weekday. They won't be able to attend the ceremony. We can't just close the center and there aren't enough part timers yet to fill in."

"I figured we'd have a formal ceremony later. This is just paperwork," Case said flippantly as he took a bite of ice cream himself then waved the spoon back and forth between them.

"We're getting married," Gabbie said seriously.

"To me you've been my wife since you moved in here."

Gabbie's head shot up and she seemed dumbstruck.

"Aren't Claire and Charlie my kids? Even though the paperwork hasn't been signed," he explained.

"I guess."

"I wouldn't have a girl move in with me if I wasn't planning on marrying her. You're my wife. You have been. We're just making it official. And later we'll do it again with the Growing Strong mafia you work with."

"Mafia?"

Case untangled their legs and pulled Gabbie onto his lap. With her back to his chest, Case locked his arms around her waist and held her small body to his.

"You're family even though you aren't related. You've got bodies buried all over the Twin Cities from those who have wronged you, and to cross one is to cross all. Mafia."

"And you think you can handle being married to me?"

"I know I can't handle not being with you," Case said as he let his lips brush against Gabbie's neck.

Inhaling deep, he pulled in the smell of her shampoo and felt the ease that came with contentment. Gabbie's body nestled in tighter against his body and he set the bowl of ice cream down on the coffee table.

Case's left hand rested, but for a moment, on Gabbie's bare knee, then dropped slowly down her inner thigh. He allowed the pads of his fingertips to graze against her supple thigh and Gabbie inhaled deeply. As his hand reached the apex of its journey, it rested in between Gabbie's thighs and started cupping gingerly to the intersection of her legs. Pressing ever so gently, he started to massage the area in soft strokes. One pass went higher than the rest and he popped the button on the top of her shorts and with his thumb separated her zipper as he came back to her junction.

Gabbie let out a satisfying whimper when his fingers drumming lightly against her returned to the top of her panties. His long fingers inched their way under the cotton fabric and into the soft folds on the outside of her core. He teased a little, playing with her clit and her head fell back onto his shoulder, so he captured her lips with his.

Inching further, he found her entrance and gladly slid two fingers inside. Her hips rotated in rhythm with his stroking fingers.

"Are you sure the kids are asleep?" he asked when their lips parted for a second.

"Don't mention them, just take me," she moaned as he delved deeper inside and he felt her start to tighten.

Her body shifted around his fingers as she turned to face him. With a knee on each side of his hips, she let him continue stroking as she removed her top. Case's right hand now went to the strap of her white bra and slid it down the side of her arm.

"We haven't christened this room," Case said with a sly smile, removing his fingers from inside her and moving both his hands to her hips.

Gabbie gathered up the bottom of Case's shirt in her fingers and dipped her head down when they pulled up his shirt. Her tongue created a velvet trail between his slightly fading six-pack. With his shirt removed, Gabbie kissed his sternum, and then looked up at him with a devilish grin.

Delicately, she fingered the top button of his jeans until it popped free and she let the zipper glide apart. Case could feel the familiar tightening in his gut as his length reached full extension, straining against the tight cotton of his boxer briefs.

Gabbie stood up long enough to drop her shorts, pull off his jeans and underwear, and then nibble on her bottom lip. His erection stood proudly at attention seeing the curve of Gabbie's hips. She sat down at the edge of the couch by his hips. Case raised up enough to brush her raven hair to the side and kiss her neck as his fingers fumbled with the clasp of her bra. When freed from the confines of her bra, Case brought his hands to her breasts and massaged. His kisses turned to light sucking and again he heard the glorious sound of her moan.

His left hand then traveled down the center of her chest to the softness of her belly while his right thumb and index finger began rolling her now erect nipple. Gripping tightly to her stomach, he picked her up and guided her to the couch. Looking at her backside, Case let out a hungry growl, then locked his fingers tightly to her hips. It took only one plunging stroke into her wanting, slick core for her to arch her back beautifully and toss her head with a glorifying moan.

Case had discovered Gabbie's favorite positions and seemed to have learned the pace and force that made her tremble the most. Slow at first until he felt the slight gripping around his erection, then he'd increase to a rapid pounding pace that would have her screaming into a pillow as her fists would bunch up in the sheets. Inside, her core would be pulling and sucking on him to the point he thought he'd lose control. At that point he'd slow down to a snail's pace.

The action would become so intense he'd be the one growling as he'd have to bite on her shoulder to taste the sweetness of her skin mixed with the salt of her perspiration. With his erection squeezed to the point he'd think he'd never be able to get it back, he'd finally bury himself as deep as he could, then grind against her tender walls as swiftly as possible until they both exploded.

Gabbie collapsed onto the couch and Case couldn't help but lay right on top of her. She had her head turned to the side and he was still nibbling at her shoulder.

"I love you, Gabbie," he whispered.

"I caught that."

"Has the room been properly christened?"

Chapter Seventeen

Women are meant to be loved, not to be understood.

—Oscar Wilde

Gabbie had called the girls into her office early the next morning. As they all crammed into the suddenly small space, Gabbie could feel the heat on her cheeks. Looking around, Mary Beth was in the chair closest to the wall, Sarah was next to her, and finally Mandy was holding tight to the door handle as she rested against the door.

"Gabbie, we only have about ten minutes before the rush," Mary Beth said.

"I know," Gabbie gasped as she ran her fingers through her hair and rested her face in her hands. "Okay…so…"

The girls sat in silence, trying to respect that Gabbie was nervous. Gabbie's stomach was tied tight and she scanned her friends' reactions. They knew that yesterday was the custody battle. It's not like they didn't know the kids thought she was their mother. They were her best friends. They'd back her every move. She had to smile at Mandy's twisted face, showing anger instead of concern.

"Out with it," Mandy blurted.

"The custody case got extended an extra week, so next Thursday I'll need to have the day off again."

"My god," Sarah exclaimed. "How long do they need to drag this out? Case is an awesome father. What's the problem?"

"Me."

"You?" Mary Beth asked. "What's wrong with you?"

"I'm not married to him."

"And?" Mandy prodded.

"And next Thursday we're going to remedy that."

"You're getting married so he can get custody," Mandy balked.

"No."

"Then why would you do that?"

"Because then I can adopt them at the same time."

"Gabbie," Mary Beth started. "Is this what you want?"

"Yes, the judge was going to give Case custody and Case asked if I could get it too and…well the long and the short of it is we're getting married and adopting them together next week."

"What about us?" Sarah asked. "We always said we'd be in each other's weddings."

Gabbie had to smile at that. The last person she thought would be upset about not putting on a tacky dress was Sarah. But as she thought about their friendship, Sarah was the one that insisted on birthday parties. She was the one who always wanted to celebrate the anniversary of them opening Growing Strong. To her, the celebration of their life achievements was most important.

"Case said that this is just paperwork. We'll have a formal ceremony later with all of you in tow."

"Just paperwork," Mandy snapped. "It's marriage. You can't be serious. What frickin' line did you fall for this time?"

"Line…I didn't fall for a line. He doesn't *have* to marry me. The judge granted him custody. He wants me—the ugly-ass six."

"You're not a six," Mandy exclaimed. "I don't want you to settle on the first guy that—"

"Loves me. That is stupid. He loves me, Mandy," Gabbie said as she stood up and crossed to her. "Please be happy for me. I need your approval."

"He didn't ask for my blessing."

"Is that what you all want? You want him to ask you for your blessing? He'll do it. He'll do anything for me so if that's what it takes he'll do it. But I swear to God if you don't give it, I'll punch you all in the throat."

At lunch, Case showed up in his best suit with a bouquet for each member of the Growing Strong mafia as well as a hundred dollars worth of Chinese food. For Mary Beth, it was a bouquet of Casablanca lilies. For Sarah, it was Mexican sunflowers in three different shades, Mandy, white roses for peace, and finally red roses for Gabbie.

They all squeezed again into Gabbie's office. This time, Gabbie sat on Case's lap. With white folded boxes in hand, Gabbie was a nervous wreck, more because Case didn't seem to be.

"Ladies, I was told we needed to have a discussion," Case began. "I thought you all already knew how much I love and cherish your friend."

"That wasn't in question," Mary Beth replied.

"Good. If the world was perfect, we wouldn't be getting married next week in a courtroom. If it was perfect, I would have found her in high school after some ball game or waiting to see a movie or buying pistachio ice cream at Cub, but I didn't. If I had I could've saved her from meeting Kirk, I would have seen all your mad skills when you still had them," Case teased.

"Not the way to win us over, Case," Sarah warned.

"I pick Gabbie because I love her. I've never broken a promise to Gabbie, and I don't plan on doing it now. Marrying her now is a technicality. We'll have another ceremony and big party so Sarah can dance on a table."

"I don't like the term technicality," Mandy growled. "It seems like it's just something to do, like buying insurance."

"I say technicality because to me she's been my wife for months now. I've been devoted to her completely. Can I please have your blessings? I love her and want to marry her without a cloud over our ceremony."

Mary Beth, Sarah, and Mandy all looked at each other. The secret telepathy they all seemed to possess had Gabbie nervous. She could see Mandy was holding out her blessing.

"I love him," Gabbie said. "He's never tried to separate us. You'll all get a new niece and nephew."

"Maybe more than one," Case cooed into Gabbie's ear as he hugged her tight.

"Maybe."

Mary Beth was the first to stand up and walk behind Gabbie's desk to hug Case and Gabbie. Then Sarah added to the pile up. Mandy stayed glued to the door.

"Come on Ms. Mand," Case said and gave Mandy a knowing look that confused Gabbie. "Just say it's okay that I marry your best friend."

"Only if I get to be the maid of honor, even though it's in a courtroom."

"Yes. We need at least one representative from the Growing Strong mafia present."

"The what?" Mary Beth asked. "Never mind. Welcome to the family, Case."

* * * *

Mandy finished applying Gabbie's makeup in the bathroom of the family court building. Gabbie gazed into the mirror and wished it was full length so she could see the whole dress that the girls had helped her pick out over the weekend—a simple white mermaid style satin dress that hugged the curves Case loved so much.

Her nails had a French manicure and her hair was loosely pulled back on the right side with a jewel-encrusted comb. A tightly wrapped bouquet of red and white roses tied with satin ribbon sat on the counter waiting to finalize the ensemble. Mandy surveyed her makeover. Satisfied that Gabbie looked appropriate, she shifted her own fire engine red halter sundress with white trim.

"Last chance," Mandy said, looking at her cell phone for the time.

"For what?"

"To runaway."

"I don't want to runaway."

Gabbie looked at a Mandy's disappointed downturned face.

"What's wrong, Mandy? Can't you just be happy for me?"

"I am. It's just…"

Gabbie knew what was wrong with Mandy. The same thing that made their relationship so strong also tore it apart. The worst part was hurting her best friend although Gabbie didn't know how many times she'd have to say the same thing for Mandy to understand. In many ways they were closer than lovers could be and Gabbie didn't understand why Mandy felt that physical intimacy could strengthen a bond that had been forged over almost twenty years.

"You thought I'd change my mind about you."

Mandy's eyes snapped up to meet Gabbie's.

"I can't be what I'm not, and I love you too much to pretend. I love him. I love his kids. They're the family I want."

Mandy wrapped her arms around Gabbie and hugged her as she stifled the normally absent sobs.

"You'll always be my best friend, right?" Mandy croaked.

"Of course. I'll need your freaky sex advice so I can keep my man interested."

"No, you don't, that man gets turned on when he knows he's within fifty feet of you," Mandy said as they finally released from their hug.

"It's the cross I bare being so damn sexy," Gabbie replied, righting her dress.

When they exited the bathroom, Gabbie's father was there in his best suit and they all entered the gallery of the courtroom, where Case was standing with his lawyer in front of the judge. The smile on Case's face made Gabbie's heart warm. He was wearing his tailor made suit again. She couldn't help but lick her lips, seeing his broad shoulders and firm chest filling out the fabric.

Gabbie's father and Mandy escorted her to Case and the judge who was standing in front of his bench. Passing her roses to Mandy, Gabbie turned to Case and intertwined their fingers.

"You two ready?" he asked.

"More than," Case said.

As the judge performed the ceremony, Gabbie's heart pounded hard in her chest. She looked at Case and his amazing dark mahogany eyes. His goatee was perfectly trimmed, surrounding his lips with the light red tint under the brown shade. The memory of what those lips had done to Gabbie over the last few months sent a shiver through her spine.

"Gabrielle Vaulst, do you take Case Thomas to have and hold from this day forward?"

With a smile on her face Gabbie happily replied, "I do."

"Then with the power invested in me by the state of Minnesota, I now pronounce you husband and wife. For some reason, I don't think I'll need to say what you're allowed to do next."

"No sir," Case said as he slid both hands on Gabbie's face and brought her soft lips to his.

When Case's lips met hers, instantly her tongue glided and met his as her arms wrapped around his neck. His thumbs stroked her cheeks and Claire and Charlie sat at their feet.

"Ugh mama 'nuf 'ready," Claire exclaimed.

"I'll never get enough," Gabbie whispered to Case, who chuckled at Claire's statement.

"Alright, time to step behind the bench and get the second half of this proceeding completed."

"I have something to say about that," Gwen said and everyone turned to see she was standing on the edge of the gallery with Kirk in tow.

Chapter Eighteen

"Facts do not cease to exist because they are ignored."

—Aldous Huxley

"Mrs. Harris, you really want to help out Washington County's deficit because I feel you'll be paying some contempt fees. I've already ruled against you," the judge warned as he walked behind his bench and sat down.

Case's jaw was clenched when he picked up Charlie and Gabbie's dad picked up Claire. Mandy passed Gabbie back her bouquet and took Charlie from Case as she leaned in and assured him that he'd be safe.

"That bitch comes within five feet of your kids and I'll cut her," Mandy whispered.

"Thanks, little sister."

"My client would like you to reconsider," Gwen's attorney asserted. "We have uncovered some disturbing character issues with both Mr. and now Mrs. Thomas and feel they are unfit to parent the minor children in question."

Ron leaned in to have a private conference with Case. "What is he talking about?" Ron asked in a low tone.

"I decked the skinny guy standing next to Gwen, but I don't know what he could have to say about Gabbie."

"Tell me what happened now," Ron growled.

"He was calling Gabbie a whore and making other degrading comments about her."

"Does she have a questionable sexual past?"

"No. Why?"

161

"Sex and violence. The only reason you could lose them."

"Seriously? That guy is a predator that nearly destroyed Gabbie in high school, and he could take away my kids?"

Case turned to Gabbie, who had tears in her eyes. She'd returned to that quiet girl in Como again. If for no other reason than Gabbie's demeanor, did Case want to not only kick Kirk's ass again, but his Aunt Gwen was moving up on the list of bodies to be buried by Mandy. Behind him, Mandy hissed at Kirk.

"Haven't you done enough to her? When will you stop?"

Kirk smirked in satisfaction, and Case was about to jump up and smack it off his face when Gabbie placed her hand on his. He turned and saw she was back. Her gray eyes were sparkling even with the tears that had pooled, but the strength he'd come to know from her was there.

"Come forward and state your case," the judge ordered. "You have two minutes before your client starts pulling out her checkbook."

"Yes, sir. Upon further review of the claimant's history, we found that he has a history of violence that started when he was in junior high and has continued as recently as a few months ago. In addition, we're finding that Mrs. Thomas' sexual history is also questionable."

"It's funny that it wasn't discovered by the social worker who dug that far."

"Mr. Thomas' father was an attorney in good standing. We all know how certain minor infractions can disappear from permanent records."

"Are you accusing one of the decedents of falsifying records?"

"I'm suggesting behavior issues may have been...altered to assist in his securing a scholarship."

"Mr. Howard, do you have any explanation?"

"Mr. Thomas got in scuffles at school when he was in the..." Ron looked at Case to get the correct grade. Both Ron and Case's father had worked with the school district to resolve the situation years ago. Case raised seven fingers and Ron continued. "Seventh grade. Neither he nor the other boy ever had any injuries—not even a bruise. Mostly they were verbal confrontations until one day they escalated. Both boys were suspended during which Mr. Thomas served a community service sentence imposed by his parents at the Dorothy Day Center. Since then, he has not had a confrontation that resulted in suspension or police involvement."

Ron looked at Case, who nodded in agreement.

"Mr. Devenshire?" the judge asked Gwen's attorney.

"No formal charges were brought from his attack of my client, but we do have witnesses to show it was an unprovoked assault that occurred when Mr. Marshall was at work."

Case clutched his fists and pressed against his leg to stifle a yell. Control. That's what he needed because he couldn't give in to his rage. Ron suddenly stood up.

"I'd like to have Mr. Marshall sworn in to testify concerning these accusations," Ron said. "Right now we have one unreliable story brought by a woman who's already been proven unfit to care for the two minor children in question."

"I agree," the judge said. "I've seen no reason to change my ruling based on a rumor. Mr. Marshall, if you wouldn't mind."

"No sir," Kirk said as he stepped into the witness stand and took the oath.

"Give me the Reader's Digest edition, Case," Ron said as he leaned in toward Case.

"He wouldn't stop swearing in front of the kids and calling Gabbie a whore."

"How many men have you been with, Gabbie?" Ron asked and Case growled in outrage.

"Two," she said, her voice shaking and face pale. "Only two. One too many it would seem."

"Two and he calls you a whore. I need to know everything."

"He lied in high school about others. But I swear it's only him and Case."

The judge interrupted their meeting. "Mr. Howard, I understand this witness was sprung on you, but have you discussed with your client enough to get this concluded today?"

"Yes sir," Ron said as he stood up. "Mr. Marshall, can you tell me how you know the claimant, Mr. Thomas, in this case?"

"He's engaged...well married to my ex-girlfriend. I've only met him once briefly."

"And what happened when you met him?"

"He punched me out."

"Why would he do that? Did he just walk up to you and punch you?"

"I think he was jealous because Gabbie and I were talking...you know, reminiscing about the good old times."

"Good times? You and her parted as friends."

"I would say so."

"Asshole. Lying asshole," Mandy screamed from the gallery.

"There will be no outbursts in my courtroom."

"I'm only doing it because she can't," Mandy growled. "She has to sit here and take his lies just like in high school because he has her trapped, Your Honor. In high school he said that she made up their relationship—that the five months they were together was all in her head and now he sits here under oath talking about how they were together. If Case hit him, he deserved it."

"He says naughy words," Claire said following 'Aunt' Mandy's lead.

"What was that, little one?" the judge asked.

"Daddy says not to says naughy words to me and Arlie," Claire continued her tattling tale. "Mama says Daddy no naughy 'cuz he naughy." Claire pointed directly at Kirk.

"He makes Mama cry," Charlie added. "He naughy boy."

"Did you make Mrs. Thomas cry?" the judge asked.

"You're listening to two lying brats?"

"You're a surprise witness. They couldn't have been coached. And two-year-olds aren't predisposed to lying. Answer the question."

"Yeah, me and the guy got into it. I was talking to Gabbie and he interrupted. I don't like people in my personal space."

"Who stepped into whose personal space?" Case snapped. "You stepped into mine after I had told you three times to not swear in front of my children."

"Okay, okay," the judge said. "No more outbursts, even from you two," he said to Claire and Charlie.

"Did you use foul language in front of the two minor children in question?" Ron asked, getting back on track.

"Yeah, I probably said a few swear words, but—"

"You work a children's amusement park. Is that not correct?"

"Yes, but—"

"So it wasn't just these children you were being inappropriate around?"

Kirk tried to answer, but Ron kept going.

"Do you usually use inappropriate language around minors? Or was it just because Mr. Thomas agitated you?"

"Yeah, because he made me mad."

"How'd he make you mad?"

"He was acting like he was some big thing and I wasn't. And like Gabbie was some thing too."

"And Mrs. Thomas isn't appropriate to raise children?"

"I don't know about that. I mean she's a babysitter for a living, but her nighttime activities should be looked into."

"You have knowledge of Mrs. Thomas being inappropriate?"

"She might have changed, but when I knew her—"

"In high school you knew her?"

"You could say that."

"You said you dated, but in high school you said you didn't."

"You know how it is. Gotta keep my options open."

"So you lied in high school about your relationship?"

"I guess."

"But you say Mrs. Thomas might have grown up since then, have you?"

"What do you mean?"

"Are you still a liar?"

"I'm not a liar."

"You just admitted you were. Now what about Mrs. Thomas' behavior makes you think she might not create an appropriate environment for the minor children?"

"She was a little loose in high school."

"How was that?"

"She had sex with a lot of guys and didn't care who was watching."

Gabbie squirmed in her seat and now Case regretted the night before graduation. He could see she was embarrassed and couldn't help feeling slightly responsible. He leaned over to whisper in her ear.

"I love you."

She gave a nervous smile.

"And that was in high school?" Ron asked.

"Yes," Kirk said with a smile. "I couldn't imagine her appetite has changed."

"And high school is where you liked to lie about your relationship with Mrs. Thomas?"

Kirk got nervous, and then tried to regain his composure.

"Um…I…"

"Never mind. I don't think you'll be able to figure out if you were lying then or now. You swore at Mr. Thomas' children and made accusations about his fiancée's virtue and all he did was hit you? Once? Or multiple times?"

"Once."

"So he didn't repeatedly hit you?"

"No."

"I'd have hit you multiple times—"

"Objection." Mr. Devenshire said aghast.

"Sustained."

"Sorry, Your Honor, withdrawn. He stopped at one hit. Why was that?"

"I don't know."

"Do you think it was because he didn't want to have his children see him assault you?"

"Objection. The witness has no way of knowing the state of mind of the claimant," Mr. Devenshire moaned in annoyance.

"Sustained. Let him tell his own story."

"Is it possible that he was avoiding having his children see him assault you?"

"It was a little late then. I was already on the ground."

"He could have kicked or stomped you."

"Objection, leading."

"Sustained. Mr. Howard that's my last warning to you," the judge said as he raised his left eyebrow.

"From the position you were in on the ground, could Mr. Thomas easily kick or stomp on you to injure you further?"

166

"Yes."

"Did he?"

"No."

"Did anyone you work with come to your aid?"

"No."

"Why not?"

"Maybe they were afraid."

"You didn't ask?"

"No."

"Did you try to fight back?"

"I wanted to, but you know…"

"No I don't. Why didn't you hit back?"

"Um."

"I think you didn't hit him back because you knew you were wrong."

"Objection. Is Mr. Howard testifying or cross-examining?"

"Sorry, Your Honor. I'll rephrase. Did you feel that you were the one who started the disagreement?"

"I wouldn't say that."

"Wouldn't you? You've admitted you lied about Mrs. Thomas in high school, swore not only in front of the minor children in question, but a park full of minors. Why didn't you hit him back?"

Kirk shifted in the witness stand and Case didn't know what was going on, but this testimony wasn't going to challenge his parental rights.

"We'll get back to it. How did Mrs. Harris find you?"

"Who?"

"Mrs. Harris?" Ron asked, again pointing to Gwen.

"Oh, I tried getting Gabbie's attention as Mrs. Harris was leaving so she knew I knew Gabbie."

"When was that?"

"Last week here."

"Here? Why were you here?"

"I had some papers to file."

"About what?"

"Huh?"

"What papers were you filing?"

"It was more…um…I had a hearing."

"About what?"

"Objection, Your Honor. What Mr. Marshall was or wasn't doing in the courthouse is not relevant. This is a public building," Gwen's attorney said.

"Overruled. You may answer the question, Mr. Marshall."

"A girl charged me with a domestic, but it's nothing."

"Domestic abuse is nothing?" Ron queried and tried to stifle a smile.

"It was a misunderstanding between me and her."

"Did you hit her?"

Kirk didn't answer.

"Closed fist or open?"

Kirk started to furrow his brow.

"I have to object again, Your Honor," Mr. Devenshire said.

"I'm sure you do. Overruled."

"Back to why you didn't hit Mr. Thomas, since you've all but admitted you have no problem hitting a woman—"

"I didn't say that," Kirk snipped.

"Oh right, you didn't answer my question. When you hit the woman who accused you of domestic assault, was it a closed or open fist? Did you hit her harder or with the same force that Mr. Thomas did you? I know if I were to hit a woman, I'd probably ease up a little on her verses a man—"

"Objection!"

"I did what you said," Kirk spat at Gwen. "I'm not the one on trial here, but I know what I say could be used in my own case. I don't care if she gets the kids and no amount money is going to change that."

"Money?" the judge asked. "Did Mrs. Harris—"

"She offered me five grand to testify about how Gabbie slept with a bunch of guys in high school and what that guy did to me at work. He did hit me and I didn't hit back because I could see in his eyes that he'd kill me. I think he saw me as a threat to his family and there was no way I'd win when a man's family's threatened."

"Mrs. Harris, five thousand seems excessive for a contempt fee, but since you were planning on making that expenditure anyway, I'll make an exception. You can drop the check off with the clerk. These children are still your relation, but if I were you, Mr. Thomas, I'd think long and hard before I'd host a family reunion."

Gabbie turned to Case and wrapped her arms around his neck. It was over. Gwen was no longer a threat.

"Back to the matter at hand. The minor children will maintain the name of Charles Isaac Thomas and Claire Alisha Thomas."

Gabbie stifled the giggle she got every time she thought about the twin's initials. CIT and CAT, Case slapped at her leg to stop her. He said his parents should have learned the lesson of initials when they gave him Ulysses as a middle name, but they said it was his grandfather's name and he should just be proud of it.

"Let's get this underway," the judge said as Case and Gabbie stood to become the legal parents of Charlie and Claire.

Epilogue

"I'm starting to see players copy what I do. I'm flattered."

—*Dennis Rodman*

Ten years later

"You've got to be kidding me!" Claire screeched at the ref after he called a foul on her. "Are you blind? That wasn't a charge."

"Claire, calm down," Gabbie snapped from the stands as she held her two-year-old daughter Cassandra on her lap while her seven-year-old-son Christian laughed.

"Claire's gonna get it."

"You've missed at least seven travels that I've seen so far. You do understand about the pivot foot, right?" Claire continued on her tirade. "She didn't have one foot planted let alone two. This isn't rec. It's traveling. Where'da learn to ref?"

Case stood with his arms crossed and waited for the inevitable technical. He hated to sit Claire, not because she was his daughter, but because she was his best two-guard.

The ref's whistle blew as he held his hands to form a T and Case looked at the girls on his team and pulled Megan to replace Claire, who was coming off the court with her hands still flying out of control.

Case wrapped his arms around her and buried her face in his chest to muffle her outrage. He then looked at Gabbie and mouthed the words *your daughter* in frustration.

It wasn't a charge, Claire was right. The girl hadn't had her feet

170

planted when Claire plowed into her. But then again, Claire did lower her shoulder, thinking she'd have gotten to the free throw line if nothing else.

Gabbie couldn't help but smile when she looked at Claire acting just like she did when she played basketball. Claire sat at the end of the bench still arguing the call with Charlie, who was taking stats. Charlie was much more like his father—calm, cool and collected in games. He tried to ignore his sister and focus on the notebook in front of him. Case was lost in the game, pulling girls up and holding them by the upper arm as he pointed out how, once subbed in, they could make the necessary adjustments.

Christian and Cassandra both were playing with toys as the Thomas family had taken up a substantial portion of the stands in the East Ridge gym this tournament.

Every once in a while, Gabbie thought about what Gwen had said the last time she talked to Gabbie—that Claire and Charlie would never see themselves in her. Case never knew that Gwen had said that and yet it was days like today when he pointed out how Claire was her daughter that destroyed any fear that Gwen was right.

After the game, Case talked to the parents who complained that their kids didn't get enough minutes or why he did this or that. Case had stopped defending his coaching strategies when the kids were in third grade. It was only the new parents that hadn't caught on yet. All the kids had a first place trophy, whether they played two minutes or forty. They'd all gotten them to the championship round and next week he hoped to do the same with Charlie's team.

But at the end of every tournament, all he wanted was to hold Gabbie and tell her he loved her. And that's exactly what he did.

THE END

About the Author

Michel Prince is an author who graduated with a bachelor degree in History and Political Science. Michel writes young adult and adult paranormal romance as well as contemporary romance.

With characters yelling "It's my turn, damn it!!!" She tries to explain to them that alas, she can only type a hundred and twenty words a minute and they will have wait their turn. She knows eventually they find their way out of her head and to her fingertips and she looks forward to sharing them with you.

When Michel can suppress the voices in her head she can be found at a scouting event or cheering for her son in a variety of sports. She would like to thank her family for always being in her corner, and especially her husband for supporting her every dream and never letting her give up.

Michel has been awarded Elite Status with Rebel Ink Press in 2013, the service award for her local RWA chapter Midwest Fiction Writers in 2013 and 2014, won Sweetest Romance at IREA and is a PAN member of RWA. She lives in the Twin Cities with her husband, son, and dog, Bolt.

You may contact the author at:

www.michelprincebooks.com
www.facebook.com/michelprincebooks
https://twitter.com/michelprince1